'THAT WERE LIKE THIS HERE'

Country Goings-on

Roger Anthony Freeman

MALTHOUSE PRESS
1996

First published by Malthouse Press, 1996.

ISBN 0 9522355 4 4

British Library Cataloguing-in-Publication Data.

A catalogue record for this book is
available from the British Library.

Illustrations by Mark Guthrie.

Printed in Great Britain by
The Ipswich Book Company Ltd.,
The Drift, Nacton Road, Ipswich.

Contents

Preface

'That were like this here' is one of the once familiar colloquial expressions with which an East Anglian countryman would preface an anecdote or tale. Language changes quickly in the late twentieth century, chiefly through the impact of broadcast voices from the electronic media which regularly penetrate most households. One suspects an overall leavening is taking place and that local accent and vernacular will eventually disappear. On the other hand, gossiping and storytelling have permanency, a natural human delight, and there will always be those happy to recount the goings-on of their locality. The following tales from an East Anglian village feature many of the same characters who appear in *I Mind The Time* and *As I Was A-Saying*, titles taken from other colloquialisms. Therefore it is appropriate that the title of this third book should be in the same vein, conveying the nature of the stories, 'that it were like this here'.

Roger Anthony Freeman.

Change - An Introduction

The East Anglian parish is not what it was: but then, is any place? Change is not always welcome, particularly when it involves a familiar landscape. For example, the fall of a fine long standing oak in a raging gale may be an unfortunate happening but to those for whom that tree has long been a visual part of everyday life its departure is another reminder that there is no such thing as true permanency. All horizons eventually change, if some only exceedingly slowly. In recent times the change in the country villages of this region, both visually and socially, has been far from slow.

Ours is an overcrowded island where humankind has left little of the natural world unsullied. Each year some twenty-five thousand acres of green fields disappear under houses, factories, roads and the like, and the rate has been accelerating. The more affluent members of society, intent on a greater degree of isolation from their fellows, seek rural habitation, now made easily accessible by the kingpin of late twentieth century life, the motor car. Thus the whole nature of the English countryside has been transformed.

Villages once based almost entirely around the agricultural economy become living spaces for people whose livelihoods are chiefly in the towns and cities. The plentiful farms and smallholdings of the early years of the century are no more. The financial pressures on agriculture have seen the small farming enterprises removed, a progressive situation where yesterday's large farm is today's small farm. The survivors are the dedicated and the wily, but increasingly agriculture is becoming the domain of large businesses controlling the cultivation of thousands of acres or vast numbers of livestock.

Nowhere has this change been more evident than in East Anglia, once considered the domain of rough peasants but in the late twentieth century a desirable location for country living. Of the twenty-five or so houses in the hamlet where I lived as a boy, only one remains in the occupation of the same family. The rest, once all humble abodes occupied by labourers, artisans or village pensioners, are now the renovated homes of middle-class immigrants from some conurbation or other. In another part of the parish a new estate has been built, the occupiers commuting elsewhere to earn their keep.

While change may be resented, the old village folk who remain have a largely philosophical attitude towards the newcomers. Not expecting them to endure; as if aliens from another planet who will soon move on. Indeed, most do not stay for many years before moving to pastures new. With the younger people this may be allied to employment and career opportunities, although society in general is now of a far more itinerant nature than in the early part of this century. Perhaps the only truly hostile voice is that of a fit, craggy nonagenarian who worked on this farm for the best part of a half-century. As Rue always tended to view anyone from an adjoining parish as a foreigner, newcomers from the towns are an aversion he has never come to terms with, and I doubt ever will. Even so, this did not dissuade him from using the occasional personal anecdote in soliciting the odd pint from these people. Obstinacy and chauvinism are Rue's well-known attributes, which don't seem to be mellowed by great age.

Whereas the newcomers are of alien status in Rue's conversation, they tend to be ignored by the other notable village elder, Harry Newson, who for as long as I can remember has been referred to as Old Newson by all, even his contemporaries. This includes Rue, who can give him a few years. The supreme raconteur and gossip of the neighbourhood, old Newson thrives on the past which allows him more than a little licence with his anecdotes simply because there are now few of his generation around to challenge the exaggerated detail. His tales reveal an indifference to the changes which have overtaken the village, as if the scene were much as it was in the past. That old Newson has survived in good health for so long is surprising to those of us who know the lethal nature of his home distillations from a wide array of vegetation, roots, fruits and fungi.

Indifference also appears to be the attitude of Archie, another pensioner and long-time employee on our farm. A mild man, he always seems to take everything in his stride and accepts the gradual disappearance of the old days and ways. But then the arrival of the newcomers has been to his benefit, with cash from jobbing gardening that the taxman doesn't know anything about. His only whiff of nostalgia to come my way was comment on the renovation of the cottage where Wully lived for many a year: "Them new folk haven't half buggered around with owd Wully's place. Seems nobody today can leave well alone."

Wully was yet another one-time employee, a small fellow with a short fuse when things went wrong. Now long gone to the churchyard, though where he is therein I know not, for a stone marker was never erected on the spot. This is not as sad as it may seem, for Wully's frugality would have abhorred any of his savings being used for such a purpose.

The two who currently work on the farm, Tim and Toby, are of much younger generations and have no problem living next door to an interior designer and a computer technician, even if in comparison the newcomers have somewhat elevated lifestyles. Tim, who likes a regular pint, has, like Rue, found a receptive audience among recent settlers for accounts of village bygones. Sure winners are the exploits of Nasty, petty thief and rogue.

I doubt that Tim is old enough to have known Nasty, who, having alienated just about everybody in the district, moved on to perform his villainy elsewhere. Most listeners find it unbelievable that anyone was known as Nasty to his face or that the character concerned would appear to revel in the epithet by using it himself: "My name is Nasty.

But I ain't!" was a frequent introduction. He became something of an infamous legend in his own time. Few people can now remember what his real names were; and I am not one of them.

Of the score of farms and smallholdings in the parish which flourished during the Hitler war, the major point of demarcation in this century, only ours and Billy Hastings' survive in the same ownership. The Guv'nor, as my father was known, did not make old bones, but Billy Hastings survived well into his eighties, still refusing to hand over the reins to a son who had himself retired by the time Billy finally popped off. A third-generation partnership keeps the old place going but I wonder for how much longer with the ever-increasing pressures on agriculture.

Farms are not the only businesses to decline in numbers. In recent years the village baker, the grocer and the dairy have all sold up. So have all but one of the little general shops. The newcomers take their custom to those grand establishments Tesco, Sainsbury, and Asda, all on the outskirts of the towns. So also do most of the indigenous villagers; they have little choice other than to do the same. Gone too are the blacksmith, the builder, the plumber and the local garage, all killed off by the big concerns. Yet incredibly the village street can support a boutique, delicatessen, ladies' beauty salon and other specialist businesses that once were difficult to find even in the nearest town.

So we who tend to think of the three thousand acres of this parish as 'our village' have had to acknowledge change and come to appreciate that it is no longer the entity of countryfolk that it was. The families which had been around for generations are now dispersed or submerged by the majority of urban immigrants. Perhaps old Newson's attitude is the right one: if you consider the past richer, then indulge in its memory. Taking this a step further I commit some of his tales and several of mine to print. Those which follow are mostly from long-gone days, and a few are more recent. If they raise a laugh or two with those we old 'uns call the newcomers, then so much the better.

Pokey Potts

I was about to post a letter in the pillarbox near old Newson's cottage, when a motorised invalid carriage passed by. Hadn't seen one for ages, and it set me thinking about a character we had in the district when I was a boy. Only had one leg. Just couldn't think of his name. If I had a mental block I knew that the grinning apparition that had shuffled up to his garden gate would know the answer.

"Evening Mr. Newson. What was that fellow called who used to zip around here in a hand-cranked, three-wheel invalid carriage?" Of course, I was playing into the veteran gossip's clutches, for the answer was sure to entail a potted history of the individual in question. But what the hell, I hadn't anything much to do that evening.

"Surprised you don't remember, him havin' such a reputation. But then he were mostly afore your time; he been gone a good while now; back in the 'sixties I reckon", was old Newson's reflective response. "Been wantin' to catch yer," he continued. "Like yer to have a sip of my last year's mangold. Best I've made for many a moon."

Having experienced the potency of old Newson's home-made wine in the past, my guard was raised: "Just one little glass then: only one. I must keep a clear head. I'm driving later this evening." Which was untrue but, hopefully, an effective bar.

"No, I won't tempt yer with anything else. Now do you come in awhile and I'll tell yer about him whose name you've forgot."

The garden gate opened and closed behind, I followed my host through the rose arch into his cottage. The interior of the kitchen appeared much as it had always been in my memory, with the bracket clock on the wall, black range stove and scrubbed elm table and chairs. The only concessions to domestic progress were the water tap over the stone sink, electric lights and kettle.

A chair was indicated and I sat down while old Newson removed two small glasses and a large wine bottle from a wall cupboard.

"Now then, try this."

I tried. It was surprisingly good; neither too sweet nor with the bitter edge that so often invades mangold wine. "Very nice. You've done a good job with this one".

Old Newson beamed: "Thought you'd like it. Now then: Pokey Potts. That's who yer were thinkin' of, weren't it?"

"Yes, that's right; Pokey Potts. As a boy I remember trying to race him on my bike. He really did push that carriage along, didn't he. Must have had enormous strength in his arms considering the speed at which he worked those hand-cranks," I reminisced.

"He were a powerful fellow, no doubt. Reckon thas why the women use to run after him. They goes for the big strappin' blokes, not the pingly ones like you and me."

Having never considered my stature all that wanting, and noting old Newson's present portly form, it was evident that our notions of what was pingly were not the same. However, I could sense old Newson was eager to deliver one of his biographical accounts so the invitation was delivered with: "Never heard he was a ladies' man. Really never knew much about him apart from him having one leg."

"Ladies' man ! Don't think there's been one round here since to match owd Pokey. Some say it were because he were taking them 'African dizzy-aks' what give a fellow more of them . . . what they called?"

"Hormones," I obliged.

The narrator gave me a quizzical look: "Perhaps they do. But what's that got to do with it?"

Sometimes it is difficult to know if Harry Newson really doesn't know the meaning of words or is just playing for laughs. Happily he didn't pursue the matter, for he was now intent on his story.

"Thas how he come to lose his leg. People think that happened in the

First World War and Pokey never told 'em any different. What really happened was that he were carryin' on with a woodsman's wife up Ipswich way. The woodsman come home early and caught 'em you know what. Let fly with his axe and took Pokey's left leg clean off – only he weren't aimin' for that. You'd think that would have cooled Pokey down. Not a bit; if anything he were worse. And what's more, that didn't put the women off one little bit. When he got that hand-cranked invalid carriage there were no stoppin' him; he were here, there and everywhere." One rarely knows when fancy replaces fact in many of old Newson's case histories. Yet while it was difficult to take much of the current offering seriously, I was curious to hear more of this one-legged womaniser; and I was most certainly going to.

"Course, he had a wooden leg fitted and he could soon hop around on that without his crutches, he were a clever fellow. That wooden leg would unscrew, so he had another made with a pointed iron dibber on the bottom that he could screw in when he wanted. Now between the wars all tater and greens planting was still done by hand, a rare slow job. What Pokey did was go round all the farmers what grew taters and greens offerin' to make holes with the dibber on his wooden leg. Once the owd farmers had seen what he could do he got plenty of work dabbin'. With a crutch under his left arm he could swing that dibber and dab it in a regular eighteen inches apart, or what was wanted, all the way up a field, and keep the row as straight as a rule. You should have seen him go; he'd cover an acre in next to no time, dabbin' with his dibber and every row as neat and even as you could want. All the owd gals that usually did the job had to do then was pop the taters or sprouts in the holes. They reckoned that with Pokey dabbin' the job was done three times as fast. Thas how he came to get the name Pokey. There was one condition that Pokey made. He wouldn't have the plantin' women in the field until he had finished dabbin' with his dibber. He bein' like he was, if he caught sight of the owd gals a bendin' and a boppin' he couldn't keep his rows straight; that upset him so he'd be a swervin' all over the place."

"How was he paid?" I queried. "By the acre ?"

"By the hole or by so many holes to the acre. Some places he went they only wanted a small plot dabbed, so that were done by the hole at a farthing a go. He didn't give any free dabs: on the other hand he wouldn't cheat. Once Pokey did a half acre for Isaac Brown, that tight owd beggar up Holton way. When he went to get his pay owd Brown wanted to cut him down a halfpenny 'cause he said there were two holes short of the number Pokey said there'd be to fill the plot when they made a deal. That proper upset Pokey. He told owd Brown if he didn't pay up he'd get the two extra holes but he'd be the only man around these parts with three in his rear end. "Pokey had a rare temper. That didn't do to upset him. He were in the Anchor one night and some bloke were a ribbin' him by sayin' he charged too much for dabbin' his wife's garden. Pokey goes outside, screws in his dibber and punctures all the tyres on the fellow's car. Then tells him he's got four holes for free. Reckon he didn't charge for all the dabbin' he did for his gal friends. He'd be dabbin' away in three or four different back gardens in a day, he would. Spent a lot of time with a gentry woman out Hadleigh way and I doubt he were there just to use his dibber. They likes a bit of rough do some of these hoity-toity owd gals. Anyways, this one had an aluminium leg made for Pokey in place of the wood one he stomped around on. Though that were lighter he didn't like it. When the war came, Hitler's one, and they was after aluminium for makin' aeroplanes, Pokey gave it to them for salvage. After that whenever a Spitfire flew over he'd holler out: 'There go my leg!' Darn fool, there weren't enough aluminium in that leg to make a pilot's joystick." "Did he ever get into trouble?" I asked; a rather equivocal question which received an ambiguous answer. "Not with them, but he did with the other." A more rational explanation followed: "Never heard of him gettin' any gals into trouble: reckon he was sterilised. By the time that trouble with little owd Hitler started Pokey was gettin' on a bit and I think all that runnin' around in his scooter and a dabbin' with his dibber were beginnin' to tell. Billy Hastings had Pokey come regular, and he always tried to get his early taters into the ground afore anyone else. Well, one day around the beginnin' of March Billy was just a seein' his cows across the Longham road for milkin' when Alice Keswick come up on her bike after charin' for someone. The owd wind were wholly a blowin' that day and Keswick was only just able to stop from runnin' into the cows, her owd brakes bein' so bad 'cause she never had them seen to. While she's a-waitin' for the cows to cross she makes time of day with Billy: 'Rare gale, Mr. Hastings. Good job that's behind me or I wouldn't be able to ride me bike. Thas properly bendin' the tree tops and your scarecrow is a flappin' so much I wonder that don't blow away'. 'Scarecrow?' says Billy. 'I ain't got no scarecrow up. That must be in someone else's field.' 'That on the left-hand bend opposite the wood is yours, ain't it? There's a scarecrow down the other end,' says Keswick.

'Yes, thas mine but thas bin got ready for early taters,' says Billy, I'll go and look when these are got to the cowshed.' You know what it was?"

Old Newson was addressing me. I could guess the answer but I feigned ignorance.

"That were Pokey. Billy had told him the field was ready earlier in the week, but there'd been a lot of rain, so Billy didn't think nothing could be done for a few days. Only Pokey thought the gale was dryin' the land out nicely so he thought he'd have a trial run. Got up the other end of the field and he gets set fast. Sunk up to his knees that were so wet. His owd dibber were right out of sight.

He was a wavin' and a hollerin' for help when Keswick went past, only she didn't hear him 'cause of the wind blowin' the sound the other way. They had a rare job gettin' Pokey out, I can tell yer. Billy and his boys managed to get Pokey's good leg free, then they twisted him round and around until he was unscrewed from his dibber. Had to come back and dig it out when the soil dried out.

Mind you, that owd field of Billy's is wet any spring. Needs drainin' but you know Billy, he'll never get around to it. Anyways, Pokey would never have got himself stuck in the owd days. Grut fellow like him would have pulled himself out. No, he was gettin' past dabbin' with his dibber. 'Sides, all them new-fangled machines for plantin' taters and greens were comin' along about that time, and soon there weren't any need for the likes of Pokey Potts. He's bin gone a long time now – and potted I dare say."

Old Newson enjoys his own wit, for he was chuckling away for a good fifteen seconds over this pun.

The fact that my Guv'nor did not grow potatoes until after the Second World War is probably the reason for my previously being unaware of Pokey's prowess. What does concern me a little is that until listening to old Newson I always thought you dibbed with your dabber, not dabbed with your dibber. Be it dabbing or dibbing, I don't think anyone is going to argue the point nowadays.

Conkers

Small boys have a habit of getting up to mischief, and bigger boys, devilment. It has always been that way I suspect, although the lenient society of the late twentieth century has allowed mischief and devilment to develop into mindless vandalism. Evidence of this is to be seen in the many security and protective measures in both town and country.

Take the bridge over the railway line on the village boundary; it now has a five-feet-high wall to make it difficult for vandals to pitch concrete blocks, steel bars and other dangerous items on to the track below. In my youth the walls of the bridge over the railway were only half the current height, affording us youngsters a marvellous location for watching the puffing steam engines of the time as they laboured up the rise out of the valley or belted down from the other direction. Such observations were usually conducted from one side of the bridge, the exact vantage point being determined by the prevailing wind, noting which way it carried the steamy smoke which billowed up every time a train passed.

Steam locomotives were a fascination for most boys, particularly for those lucky enough to have parents who could afford to buy them a Hornby train set, at the time almost a status symbol in the world of toys. A cycle ride to a bridge or level crossing in the next village was a popular out-of-school activity to watch the bright green express engines roar by and, if one were lucky, the streamlined *East Anglian*. With the coming of the Second World War all the bright green quickly disappeared under a coat of matt black paint, and we train enthusiasts had another reason for hating Adolf Hitler.

As acknowledged, not all boyhood activity was sweet innocence. On one occasion a seemingly harmless train-spotting expedition developed into a villainous escapade. Wednesday afternoon was for school sports, but if a pupil did not wish to participate in playing cricket, football or whatever, he could, with permission, have the afternoon off on condition he undertook extra classroom attendance on Saturday morning. Providing parents could give an acceptable reason why their offspring could not attend school on Saturday morning it was possible to have the Wednesday afternoon and also forgo the Saturday morning tuition. This was my fortunate position, as I didn't really care about sports or school altogether, sentiments shared with my friend Bob, who also had parents who were willing to work it so that he could miss sports and have Saturday morning off as well. We were both reluctant students.

One autumn Wednesday after leaving school at mid-day we decided to make a detour and cycle home via the railway bridge. My parents were out and Bob's were both at work, so we thought we could eat our lunchtime sandwiches while enjoying our favourite pastime. Rail traffic was somewhat slow at first, and while waiting for the next train to pass below, we noticed a bountiful horse chestnut tree in a nearby fence. It was conker season and this tree had shed many fine, firm examples. The conker on a string ritual grew and waned each autumn school term, with its inevitable collection of bruised knuckles and fingers among the participants in this strange sport. The object was to shatter your opponent's conker with a swing of your own, the surviving conker being valued by the number of its victories. The conkers in other parishes were obviously more hardy than those from the trees in mine, for I never owned more than a 'two-er' or 'three-er' (the number of its victories) whereas some boys had 'ten-ers' or even higher totals for their conkers, leading to suspicions of the nut having been baked to harden it. Naturally, it never did to suggest such cheating to a bigger boy as his conker would most likely then be used against your person.

This particular collecting occasion degenerated into a chuck-at-one-another rumpus. As being hit by a thrown conker is not the most pleasant of experiences, we agreed a cessation of hostilities and turned our attention to throwing them at passing goods trains, an act of contempt for their grubby tank engine power. Tiring of this, friend Bob came up with an attractive idea. Why not hang over the bridge parapet and drop conkers down the funnels of the locomotives as they passed below? Wonderful sport. We may have claimed to have succeeded in this venture, but I doubt any of the hundred or so conkers we dropped ever entered those belching orifices. At one point we chose to drop a few stones instead of conkers, reasoning that being heavy they would be more likely to hit the objective. Fortunately stones were not readily available, so we returned to the less harmful conkers.

Of course, to achieve our not too accurate aim from the centre of the bridge span there was no escaping being enveloped in steam and smoke from the belching monsters as they thundered underneath us. This only added to the excitement, for we endeavoured to throw the conker into the funnel and retreat quickly before the smoke reached us. Possible with a goods train lumbering up the slope, but not with an accelerating express.

Most of the afternoon was taken up with this wanton activity, greeting every train except when, to avoid reproach from a passing cyclist or vehicle driver, we reverted to being innocent spectators. During a lull as tea time was approaching I chanced to look at Bob, and saw not the podgy white face that normally surmounted his plump figure but a countenance more usually associated with coal miners. "You look like a black man," I chortled. Bob eyed me: "So do you. Your white shirt collar's gone grey!"

Hasty surveillance of my person revealed blackened hands, legs and school clothes. My thoughts immediately turned to the likely reception when my mother set eyes on me. A sinking feeling akin to fear set in. The mind worked feverishly to find some explanation of my condition that might shift the blame, but none was forthcoming. Bob was no doubt similarly troubled, for little was said as we cycled home. Two ten-year-old villains about to face execution could not have been more sombre.

In those days laundry was a laborious task for country wives, and the state of my school clothes met with the anticipated anger. A 'good hiding' was the normal parental bestowal on the culprit who had sinned as gravely as I had. My backside smarted for several days, and so did Bob's from similar retribution encountered on his return home.

We didn't give up train watching, but there were no more attempts at dropping stones or conkers down funnels and we made sure to keep well clear of all locomotive emissions.

Ironically, Bob spent most of his working life with a company that manufactured detergents, but I think that was purely coincidental and not some sort of psychological penance for the episode in misspent youth. He lives in another part of the country and I had not seen him for nearly forty years until he recently visited relations in this area. The pudginess had given way to a heavily rounded figure with an abdomen that told of regular interest in the wares of public houses. We talked of our childhood and I reminded him of that long- gone day of infamy.

"They've raised the bridge parapet another two and a half feet. You'd have to use a ladder to do it today," I said.

“That wouldn’t be a problem but it would be a waste of time,” he responded.

“Why ?” I queried.

“No funnels any more !”

The Coffin War

There have been Dewsbys in Longham for the best part of a century, and one can find fourteen of them in Longham churchyard. A well-known if not notorious member of the family, Bert Dewsby, is buried in Bergholt churchyard. Not his wife's or relatives' wish, but as a result of what came to be called the Coffin War.

Time was when most sizeable villages had a jobbing builder cum carpentry business which actually derived most income from undertaking. Our local was Tom Fenney, whose repeated saying was: "There's no more assured business than undertaking, 'cause people can't change their minds when it comes to dying." No doubt Fenney regularly took stock of those in the village soon likely to meet their Maker and planned accordingly.

People may not be able to change their minds about dying, but occasionally the law of averages does not seem to be working. Such a dearth occurred in this parish in the early 'sixties when for many months the Grim Reaper was apparently mostly engaged elsewhere. With only two funerals in 1961 Fenney was having a lean time and decided to canvass trade elsewhere.

Now it was an unwritten rule that each undertaker should keep to his traditional catchment area and not poach in that of others, so that competition was limited to the ubiquitous Co-op who operated far and wide from our nearest town. In those days the Co-op was portrayed as a big ogre about to extinguish all small businesses by unfair advantages.

A complete nonsense, of course, if eagerly exploited by the likes of Fenney when championing the cause of private enterprise at local level.

The lean year encouraged Fenney to tidy up long overdue accounts which included six lengths of three-quarter-inch board acquired by Bert Dewsby for his cattle float after six bullocks broke the tail gate while loading at a farm. Dewsby was well known for ignoring bills until pressed, and Fenney knew the only way to press was to confront the debtor in person. Having decided that 10 o'clock Sunday morning was the most opportune time to call, no livestock being hauled and the pubs not yet open, Fenney motored to Longham. The cattle float was parked in the yard and Mrs Dewsby was cleaning the front door knocker of the house.

"Bert about,Missus?"

"He is and he ain't," replied Mrs. Dewsby, wiping her podgy hands on her pinny.

"Well I was just passing and I thought he might like to settle for six boards he had for his float door that got broke when he was over at Billy Hastings' farm last year."

"Afraid you'll have to wait 'til his affairs is tidied up. He was took with a seizure last night. He's a goner, dear." There was not the slightest trace of emotion in her voice.

Tom Fenney immediately offered condolences and apologies only to be told: "The way he carried on that were bound to happen some day. The old fool wouldn't listen to me or the boys."

The apparent indifference to her husband's passing led Fenney to proffer his willingness to help with funeral arrangements should she require these services.

"I'm having the Co-op. Might as well get a divvy on him. I didn't get much out of him when he were alive except trouble."

Her acid response was sufficient to unleash Fenney's full commercial acumen: "I can do you a much better price than the Co-op, divvy and all. If you don't mind deal board I can save you a good £20 on the coffin. Probably more 'cause Bert didn't have much weight on him and I reckon we could get away with a thinner board than usual."

Whether it was a question of the widow's avarice or her frugality I know not, but a bargain was struck there and then.

"You want to run a rule over him now ?"

"Don't really think it's necessary. Still, just to be on the safe side, I will."

Fenney followed Mrs.Dewsby into the house and through to the back room. The deceased was laid out on a single bed, fully attired. A distinctive odour pervaded the place which Fenney quickly identified as a mixture of beer and bovine manure.

"Are you going to have him put into something more suitable?" Fenney enquired.

"Usually slept like that when he came in here, he might as well go out like that. I ain't a-going to change him."

"Well, I think his boots better come off, if nothing else. That old bullock muck may rot the boards." Fenney had heard Dewsby and his missus didn't get along too well, and now he could understand why.

"Be warned, Mr Fenney, that's what drink and bad company does to you. Leads into dirty ways and habits," the widow scolded.

Fenney was extravagant with his words of agreement, which was somewhat hypocritical, for while he might not have been a drunkard the undertaker was well known in our village for his regular patronage of certain inns. And while he might not have been afraid of soap and water, he was rarely free of the smell of wood varnish and glue.

Word of Bert Dewsby's demise having spread around Longham, the following morning Eddie Brackett, of Brackett and Sons, arrived at Mrs Dewsby's door. The Bracketts were to Longham, Hordsley and Bergholt what Fenney was to our parish and those to the east.

"Come to see about the arrangements for Bert's funeral."

"I've already arranged with Tom Fenney for him to do it."

Eddie Brackett was more than a little taken aback: "But Bracketts have always buried Dewsbys," he protested.

Mrs Dewsby then told him the agreed price.

"He can't do a decent job for that. He's having you on. 'Sides, your boys would want Bracketts to do it, I'm sure."

"They only come near me when they wants something, and I'm the one that's dealing with Bert. I ain't going to spend a penny more on him than I just told you."

Eddie Brackett eventually retreated a troubled man. How dare Fenney poach business on Brackett's preserves? If thoughts could kill, Tom Fenney was a dead man.

The July sun shone bright on the day of the funeral. The big black hearse, converted from a 1947 Humber saloon, was given a good polish before Tom Fenney and his three workers, all suitably attired in black, set off to collect Bert Dewsby in his cut-price coffin. Young Bramble Blake drove, with Tom Fenney beside him, while the other two, Jimmy Judd and Phil Hobbs, sat behind on improvised seating. Having collected the deceased in good time, a fortifying drink was desirable and the hearse was discreetly parked at the back of Longham King's Arms while thirsts were quenched. A fortifier was a frequent prerequisite at many a Fenney served funeral, with those few public houses in the district which had behind-the-establishment parking being the beneficiaries of the undertaker's custom.

Having imbibed, young Bramble Blake had need to go to the Gentleman's. Although 47 years old, the nickname distinguished him from his father, Old Bramble. Why the family should be blessed with Bramble no one around here remembers, only that it distinguishes them from another Blake family in the village. Nor have I any knowledge of their real first names. Be that as it may, when Young Bramble returned to the Tap Room he was somewhat agitated:

"You ain't a' gonna believe this, Tom. Someone's stole Bert Dewsby."

"Stole? What you talking about, Bram?" Tom Fenney spluttered over his pint.

"The coffin's gone. When I come out of the Gents just now I see the drape was all rucked up. So I goes across and opens the back of the hearse to straighten it. There's just four beer crates under the drape. The coffin's been took."

Fenney and the others were up and out of the Tap Room like greased lightning. It was true; four wooden beer crates and no coffin. Perhaps a practical joker had hidden it nearby, suggested Jimmy Judd. They searched high and low without success. The other customers and the landlord had seen or heard nothing suspicious – or so they said.

"Back to the workshop, boys. We'll have to get the coffin we just finished for Mrs Martin. Can't hold up the service, so we'll take that into the church and no one will be any the wiser. I'll go to the police as soon as the service is over. Dewsbys needn't know what's happened." There was more than a note of panic in Fenney's voice.

The Humber hearse went through the lanes as it had never gone before. "Step on it Bram," commanded Fenney. Bram did and the radiator was boiling when they arrived at the yard.

"Quick, screw the lid on," Fenney demanded.

"Hold hard, Tom, that ain't lined. You got to put something in otherwise that'll sound empty when we put it down or the vicar throws dirt on top," Bramble cautioned.

"No one is going to know." Even as he refuted the suggestion Fenney looked round for something suitable and his eyes came to rest on the dustbin outside his back door. "All right then. Here, quick, tip my old gal's dustbin in. She's been nagging me to empty it."

Phil Hobbs removed the dustbin lid and obliged. A mixture of kitchen waste and floor sweeping splurged on to the bottom of the coffin. The mixture included potato peelings, fish heads and other fermenting items.

"That wham a bit, boss," said Hobbs, puckering his nose.

"You trying to tell me Dewsby didn't? Here, screw the lid down and let's be off."

Once more the Humber hearse thundered out on the Longham road. Slowing at a junction, two men by the wayside removed their hats as a mark of respect, which must represent a unique happening to the contents of a dustbin. Longham church stands near the old squire's residence in the middle of his estate, the Tudor gentry wishing to appease the Good Lord. It is reached by two long tree-lined drives, and before everyman and his motor car must have entailed a good Sunday hike for the parishioners of the village proper, a mile away.

Tom Fenney looked at his watch. "Blast, we are going to be six minutes late."

When at last, radiator boiling, the Humber came to stop in the parking place beside the church, Tom Fenney did not immediately get a grasp of the situation that presented itself. When he did his normally placid complexion reddened rapidly, and as what was happening really sank in it went from red to puce. Besides three cars in the parking place there was another hearse, the Brackett and Sons hearse. From the sound of the hymn coming from the church the service was well underway. Tom Fenney was not normally given to invective but this occasion was one of the exceptions (muted here):

"That f 'ing Eddie Brackett. I should have known that was that f 'ing Brackett."

The others evidently decided this was not the time to make any comment.

"Right," exclaimed the fuming Fenney. "Get the coffin out as quietly as you can and into the churchyard. I'll show the beggar."

The service over, the bearers shouldered Bert Dewsby's coffin to the grave, the vicar leading the way. When they reached the excavation there was already a coffin in residence with a few handfuls of soil scattered on top. The Longham vicar's composure was sorely tried. He apologised to the Dewsby family saying that he could only think the grave digger had somehow forgotten to cover the last burial and dig a grave for this. It seemed the only logical explanation. Eddie Brackett could smell a rat – he could definitely smell something – but thought it wise not to express an opinion other than to declare he would admonish the grave digger, even though he knew Charlie Gaybarrow never made a mistake. In an effort to placate the Dewsbys he suggested that use be made of a grave dug at St Mary's, Bergholt, which was intended for a funeral later in the week; there would be plenty of time to get another one dug for that event. The Dewsbys were quite amenable, so long as it didn't cost any more. A telephone call to the vicar of Bergholt and off everyone went to the vacant grave in his churchyard. Not long after they were departed for Bergholt church, the methodical Charlie Gaybarrow arrived with his spade at Longham and filled the occupied grave.

When Eddie Brackett was paid by Mrs Dewsby he sent a cheque for half to Tom Fenney to cover the cost of Bert's coffin. A conciliatory move. And when Fenney next encountered Mrs Dewsby she thanked him for letting Eddie Brackett handle Bert's funeral as Bracketts had always seen to Dewsbys.

Tom Fenney simply murmured: "That's all right" and made no further comment, for earlier that day a policeman had arrived in his yard to ask if he'd had a coffin stolen recently. Fenney played innocent and asked why.

He was told the Longham vicar had been much concerned by the open grave, at first thinking it was due to some misunderstanding between the grave digger, the undertaker and himself. On checking his register he had found there was no entry for this plot, which made him even more concerned. So much so he went to the police, who brought in a team to carry out an exhumation. There was no body; some practical joker had been at work.

Fenney was wise enough not to ask if anything had been found in the coffin. There is such an offence as wasting police time, and the officers involved, who cannot have been very pleased with what they found, would probably have been very willing to press charges.

The Good Turn

There was a newcomer in *The Hollies*, the large house on the hill where Mrs Marsfield had lived for more than sixty years. Rumour held that he was something to do with a merchant bank, pots of money, judging by the amount of work carried out on the house and grounds. Name of Bokof, pronounced Boo-cough. Forbears were Russian.

We olduns nearly always resent change in the village, particularly when Mrs Marsfield's place had stood unmolested for as long as most of us can remember, until the old lady died at the venerable age of 96. Her grandchildren put the place on the market and, as expected, it was another of the new rich from the city who acquired the property.

No one abhors change more than old Rue, and his vilification of foreigners – anyone from outside the parish boundaries – is legendary. I knew I would get an earful on this latest development.

"Have you seen what's going on at Mrs. Marsfield's old place? Bloody disgraceful. They cut down that holly tree in the front. Should never have been allowed, just so him that's bought the place can have a better view from his windows. They say he's a bloody Russian name of Bugger-off or the like. Well, its a pity he don't bugger off to where he came from!"

"Boo-cough," I volunteered, despite feeling some sympathy with Rue's sentiments. It was a fine holly tree and unusually large. And there was a touch of nostalgia on remembering my youthful escapade with Nasty when he was trapped up the tree one evening while in an act of stealth. Having demolished the holly tree, the thought was that the new owner would probably rename the house. The locals were already calling it the Kremlin.

Rue continued his tirade: "I don't know what Mrs Marsfield would say if she could see what's going on. They've half gutted the house a puttin' in all those fancy things these townie dwellers can't do without. And do you see what they done all round the garden and the back paddock? Pulled out all the hawthorn hedge and put up bright white palings. That'll look more like a lunatic asylum or a public convenience than a house what's lived in by the time they've finished. I don't know what the old country's a comin' to when they lets the likes of that fellow move in. We don't want no Commies round here!"

It was no good trying to explain that because the man had Russian connections he was not necessarily a Commie or an ex-Commie. When Rue gets an idea in his head you couldn't even shift it with a bulldozer. Rue believes that Rue is never wrong.

That spring, when crop spraying was in full swing, Tim came to me with a long face: "Had a slight accident. I was coming down the hill with the sprayer and I had to pull over to let the milk lorry past. You know how narrow it is there. Had to pull in close where that Russian bloke has had all the fence taken down in front of *The Hollies*. When I was watching to see if the lorry could get by I accidentally caught my elbow on the switch that turns on the right-hand boom and sprayed part of his flower bed before I could stop it. The boom being folded up, the spray sort of went out in an arc."

Accidents will happen, and we do have public liability insurance, but I didn't relish having to approach the city newcomer and explain that what had happened was an accident and not an act of vandalism. One can get taken to court for this sort of thing. At least it was a selective weedkiller and the hope was that the plants in the flowerbed were resistant. This hope was dashed when I arrived at the scene of the incident. A whole swath of aquilegias in the centre of the bed were already hanging their heads in the warm spring sunshine, a sure indication that the herbicide had knocked them for six.

The front door of the house was opened by a trim young woman who informed me in cultivated tones that Mr. Bokof was "unavailable until the evening", the posh way of saying he was at work, jacking up his fortune still further. I explained to the young lady that I was the neighbouring farmer and that one of my men had accidentally sprayed some weedkiller on part of the flowerbed near the road. She seemed quite unmoved and instructed me to come back at 8 o'clock that evening when "Mister Bokof will be in residence." I have no idea if this young woman was housekeeper, personal assistant, wife, mistress or whatever, for to this day the status of the female contingent in that house remains a mystery - and I have personally encountered three and it is rumoured there are two more, all the right side of thirty. Even the main contributors to the village grapevine have yet to work this one out.

At 8 o'clock sharp, as bidden, I arrived at Bokof's front portal, respectably attired, if apprehensive of my reception. The door was opened by a man whom I would place as being in his late forties. Of stout build and medium height, a clean-shaven, rounded face, and balding on top. In contrast to the city suit expected, the casual slacks and sweater, plus a wide smile put me more at ease.

"Mr. Freeman? Do come in. Hear you're concerned about a free weeding of my flowerbed." All very Oxford when I had been expecting broken English and an eastern European accent. He led the way into a room which I remembered as being rather dowdy 1920s decor in Mrs. Marsfield's day. One didn't have to be a patron of Harrods to appreciate that the current furnishings would spoil the look of a few thousand pounds. Somewhat in contrast, with its heavy gilt frame was a very large portrait of a decidedly Russian-looking gentleman suspended above what had once been the open fireplace and was now a set-in drinks cabinet. Having accepted a medium sherry my inquisitiveness drew me to comment on the fur-clad gentleman with the fine-tuned beard in the picture. Mr Bokof was only too happy to explain it was his great-grandfather and that the portrait was brought out of Russia by his great uncle when escaping from the Bolsheviks in 1918. From there on I was given a family history without further questions on my part. Mr Bokof's father had been a colonel in the Red Army, and after being wounded worked as an embassy attaché. In 1950, when Mr Bokof was only two, his father defected while with a Soviet mission to France. The family joined the great uncle who had prospered in London's financial world, Mr Bokof's father being taken into the business. Mr Bokof, too, had gone into banking after Cambridge. Although born in Russia he was now a naturalised British citizen. As for the portrait of old great grandad, great uncle had no heirs so the painting had come to Mr Bokof when his benefactor died. I heard about the oppression of the Stalinist regime and his dislike of the Germans because of the destruction wrought in Russia. I couldn't help thinking this didn't quite fit in with the ostentatious Merc' outside the front door. It was extremely difficult to divert my host back to the reason for my visit. Finally, I was able to mention that our insurance would cover the damage to the flowerbed and reinforced my apologies.

"No need to worry about that. I am going to do away with that border: put it down to lawn. Going to have a brick wall built along the road boundary. That is why I had the hedge taken out. Just waiting for the builder to start. Due next week, actually. Don't give the spraying trip another thought. No harm. No problem."

This pronouncement certainly gave relief, which together with a second sherry probably accounted for my willingness to accede to Mr Bokof's following request.

"I will tell you what you can do for me as a good turn. You farmer types have guns, don't you? I have a pest in my garden I would like you to take a pot at."

I visualised rabbits on his lawn or pigeons pecking buds in the kitchen garden: "Yes, I've a .22 rifle. What's the problem?"

"You know the large pond in the garden, down near the boundary with your field - it is yours along by the willow trees? I have had it cleaned out, it was in a terrible mess, full of mud. Stocked it with fish. Natasha is an enthusiast for fish. Annoyingly an acquisitive heron keeps coming and taking the fish. We cannot persuade it to stay away. Will you shoot it for me?"

A bit taken aback I tried to evade: "Herons are a protected species aren't they? We may get into trouble with the law."

Bokof was undeterred: "My fish are going to be a protected species. One heron less will not make much difference. I am told there are far too many around. No one will know and we will certainly not say anything. You just pot it off one morning and Katinka will dispose of the corpse. She is quite hardened to that sort of thing. Doesn't bat an eyelid."

"Oh," I said, for a moment not knowing what to reply, and then attempting another let-out: "Isn't there a risk of one of the men working on your place seeing the heron shot?"

"No one here for the rest of the week apart from Katinka, Rula and Tanya. No workman until next Monday. That will give you five days. It is there every morning and if it does not see you coming it should be no problem to dispose of."

Of course, I should have had the courage there and then to give an emphatic no. Just because he had been so decent about the weedkiller on his flowerbed I'd taken an appeasing attitude. Well, perhaps the heron wouldn't come back and even if it did I could always miss it, or accidentally frighten it. The request nagged at my conscience during the next two days when, because of business appointments away from the farm, there was no opportunity to carry out the villainous deed. My concern was not so much knocking off the heron as being caught breaking the law; which reveals my cowardly nature. On Friday morning I thought I'd better show willing so crept out at six thirty with the .22 under my arm. The morning was bright and the recent growth of spring greenery provided good cover as I made my way against the hedge that runs along the field at the rear of Bokof's house. The hope that the heron was not visiting the fish pond that day was soon dashed. Through a gap in the hedge I caught sight of the grey shape, posed intently at the pond's edge, ready to spear the first fish that was foolish enough to swim near. It was our hedge, otherwise Bokof would have pulled it out as he had all those on his property and without cover the bird would have seen my approach. But strangely, having set eyes on my quarry the qualms about the morality of my mission were supplanted by the determination of the hunter. To get within range it would be necessary to drop down and crawl. The dew was no problem as I had come prepared with waterproof jacket and leggings. Edging forward carefully, hands were twice stung by emerging nettles and then jabbed by a dead thistle I'd failed to notice. The heron still stood transfixed, awaiting its prey's move into range. I could have coughed, flapped an arm or done something to alert the bird of the impending danger, but the hunter instinct prevailed and I continued to wriggle forward until reaching a position where my quarry was well within range, an easy shot. Fixed in the cross-hairs of the telescopic sight, the finger on the trigger overcame any lingering doubt. Crack! To my amazement the heron remained standing. Surely I could not have missed? Then I noticed a slight oscilation. A quick squint through the telescopic sight revealed why. The bird had no legs; just a rod entering its body. It was a plastic heron!

I am sure my face must have flushed with embarrassment. Fortunately there was no one around to see. Nevertheless, in case the shot had alerted someone in the house or garden, a hurried retreat was performed, bent low to keep well out of sight. Was this a joke at my expense? An example of the Russian sense of humour? Had Bokof deliberately set out to humiliate me for the weedkiller on his flowerbed? I mulled over such thoughts all day.

That evening the 'phone rang and a voice with a heavy foreign accent announced: "This is Rula from *The Hollies*. Mister Bokof asked me to telephone you to say he is trying a plastic heron at the fish pond.
He has been told it is a very effective way of keeping herons off. I telephoned yesterday to tell you. There was no reply and you do not have an answering machine so I could not leave a message."

Explaining that I had been away from home, I thanked her for 'phoning. She apparently did not know what had occurred that morning and I was not going to enlighten her. In fact no one was told of the incident as I did not want to become the laughing stock of the community. There was relief in being able to save face.

About a month later while chit-chatting in the post office, a young woman looking at the picture postcards in the rack must have sized up who I was. As I turned to leave she gave me a big smile: "You must be Mister Freeman, the man who shoots plastic herons. I'm Katinka from *The Hollies*. I know a bullet hole when I see one. A very good shot. We will know where to come if it doesn't work." A good smattering of eastern European accent here.

"Yes," I laughed – a very forced laugh – as a hurried exit was made, hoping the postmaster hadn't heard. Our postmaster has radar ears and it was too much to hope, for I later learned it gave the regulars at the Wheelrights Arms and the Anchor something to joke about for weeks.

The plastic heron seems to have worked. Even so my excuses are prepared should my shooting services be sought again. I'm all for international co-operation, yet I'm a little uneasy about these Russian folk. For a start, how come this Katinka is so authoritative about bullet holes?

A Bad Case Of Shock

With farm folk the veterinary is accorded a similar status to that which most of us bestow on the family doctor; a superior being possessed of life-giving skills. Over the years six different vets have served our farm for varying periods, the longest in attendance being Mr. James McTeggert. McTeggert was a hardy Scot who had deserted the lowland counties to follow the many farmers moving to kinder land in the south during the agricultural depression of the 'twenties and 'thirties. In fact, it appears that just about every Scottish farmer in the area claimed a relationship to McTeggert, but one suspects most were tenuous. If there was some canny thought that, for example, being second cousin's wife's brother might bestow cheaper services, I doubt this was achieved. McTeggert's expenditure on his homeland's favourite tipple could not have allowed room for discounts.

The single most overpowering memory of McTeggert was his whisky-laden breath, which one could not escape if keeping animals secure while he plied his trade. He was obviously aware of this discharge as on one occasion, while Wully, with fag in mouth, was holding a calf by the nose for McTeggert to dose, the veterinary advised: "You'll be putting that cigarctte out Wully or we'll both be blown to the devil". The degree of alcohol intake varied, and McTeggert very occasionally arrived at the farm completely free of whisky vapours. Such temperance was indicated by a decidedly tetchy disposition, whereas all was benevolence and patience when a dram or two had fortified his constitution. An indication of the quantity recently consumed was the speed at which he drove his car. The higher the intake the slower the Austin moved, which implies – to his credit – that he was aware of his condition. It was not unknown for the car to progress at no more than running pace after a long lunch break at the Wheelright's Arms. And even Wully, the slowest of pedallers with his flat feet, had overtaken it on his cycle on several occasions. The reader will, of course, appreciate that this was before the days of major drink-drive concern, when cars on our country roads were few and far between and the local Law was given to turning a blind eye, particularly when his cat was spayed free of charge. As far as I am aware McTeggert never got into any form of trouble while at the wheel of his car. Likewise I never heard of any deterioration in his veterinary skills as a result of his drinking. On the contrary, his work seemed all the more positive when the breath was heavily laced with his favourite malt. On more than one occasion during my youth I had been concerned as to where the surgeon's scalpel might stray while holding piglets for McTeggert to castrate, a concern that he sensed: "Don't fret laddie. I know where the pig ends and you begin."

Another peculiarity of McTeggert was that, intoxicated or sober, all his utterances were at the same level and steady pace. The voice was never raised, however fraught the situation. Apart from breath the only indication of heavy imbibing was a rather hazy realisation of what was going on around him. He might be precise in injecting into a heifer's neck vein, but while doing it he appeared to be oblivious to anything beyond the immediate area of his work. The frosty morning when the brewer's lorry ran into the ditch outside the farm gate McTeggert did not even hear the sickening crash as two cases of *Johnny Walker* smashed to pieces on the road.

Then there was the morning when a cow called Annabel was having difficulty in calving. McTeggert needed extra hands, so I called Archie into the cowshed to assist, he, apart from Clive the cowman, being the first to arrive for work that morning. Archie didn't seem too enthusiastic but followed me back into the cowshed, only to pass out as soon as he got behind the cow. "You shouldn't have got him in", said Clive, "he faints at the first sight of blood."

This was news to me. And there was only a little blood to be seen. While Clive and I were trying to revive Archie, McTeggert turned from the cow and, seeing the prostrate man in the far from salubrious gutter, advised: "Not the time to be lying down to rest man. We need your help here." It was not said in jest: McTeggert just did not comprehend the circumstances thanks to his alcoholic haze.

This particular calving was extremely difficult. A leg was round the wrong way for delivery, requiring McTeggert to reach into the uterus and turn the offending limb. Three of us on the end of a rope finally got the calf out. Not a job for the squeamish. Not pleasant for the cow either. All the same mother and progeny survived. The worst affected was Archie, who had a nasty lump where he had bumped his head when swooning, plus a large amount of undesirable gutter debris on coat and trousers.

In the afternoon of the following day Clive called me from the dairy door: "You better have a look at Annabel. I had a job to get her up. Looks lame in a front leg."

I accompanied Clive to the loose box where cow and calf were housed. As Clive had said. the cow appeared to have a painful left front leg, which was mystifying as the animal's gait appeared perfectly all right when driven to the loose box after calving. I instructed Clive to see how Annabel was next day and if there was no improvement I'd 'phone the vet.

There was no improvement. The cow seemed fine in every respect except the left front leg which it tended to hold from the ground as if tender. So I 'phoned McTeggert who duly arrived, a little sober and a little irritable, I thought. He felt the leg, could find nothing amiss, and advised it was just a sprain. A case of wait till nature took its course.

Five days later I sent for him again as there had been no improvement. This time he was more his old self, well drammed up and as happy as they come. A more thorough examination revealed no swellings, fractures or anything else that could be the cause of lameness. Even McTeggert was puzzled, although speculating it was all due to shock.

Another week went by and still no improvement. I was beginning to think this would eventually be a case for the knackers. A last resort, for Annabel was a good milker and this only her third lactation. McTeggert came again, but could still find nothing wrong: "I'll go down to the Anchor and get myself a wee dram and think what we can do." He didn't come back that day.

I think it must have been the following day when, while crossing the yard to the cowshed, I was suddenly confronted by a gypsy woman selling lucky heather: "Mister, will you be needing good luck?"

"I'm always needing good luck," I laughed. The woman was what one might call a typical Romany. A handsome, tanned, angular face with dark eyes. Black as black plaited hair packed into a bun behind and held with a red ribbon. A green wool cardigan above a long black skirt terminating just short of the tops of lace-up working man's boots, worn but polished. Her left arm supported a wide willow basket filled with white heather posies, each having tinfoil wrapped around its base. I would have placed the woman as in her early thirties. What she wore was probably her best attire. Given reddened lips, flowing hair, a flamenco dress and feminine shoes she would have been a stunner.

Her right hand clasping a rather scrawny sprig was outstretched towards me: "Buy a lucky heather and you'll have good luck, sir."

"I could do with some right now but I don't think your heather will help."

"It may, sir. What is your trouble?" The thrusting arm remained in front of me as she spoke.

"It's not really me. It's one of my cows. Gone lame."

"I know who can cure that for you. Buy a heather and I'll send him along. Only a shilling." The heather was lifted close to my face.

Perhaps it was simply to get rid of her, or maybe just that I felt generous for once. I bought the sprig and the gypsy was gone as quickly as she came. Annabel was no better that day and for no other reason than I did not know what to do with it I stuck the heather sprig over the loose box door.

My worry about losing a valuable cow made a visit to the loose box the first task each morning. Clive was already taking a peep and shook his head as I approached. Seeing the heather I joked that the gypsy's charm hadn't done much good. I was walking back across the yard and just about to go into the house, when a didicoy's vehicle came chugging through the gate.

At least that was my immediate identification of the aged Ford that had probably started life as a van but now had a wooden buck in place, a conversion that put it somewhere between a pick-up truck and a small lorry. A short, round and red-faced man climbed down from the driver's position and approached me. I cannot recall much about his dress apart from his wearing a black jacket and a widish brimmed brown hat. The expectation was a request for scrap iron. Instead, to my surprise, he asked: "You're wanting a lame cow put right?"

"Yes, but I don't think you can do anything." I did not at first connect the man with the gypsy flower seller, although this was obviously the source of his knowledge.

"Let me have a look Mister and I'll tell you if it can be done."

There was no rational thinking on my part. I just took him to the loose box, not for one moment expecting anything more than an attempt to sell me some charm. The man opened the door of the box, approached Annabel who was still lying down, and started to feel the left leg in much the same fashion that McTeggert had done. Before I could ask how he knew it was the left leg he volunteered: "As soon as I saw her I could tell it was that front one. I can cure it for you. How much is the cow worth when she's fit?"

Still somewhat taken aback by all this and not really having had time to crystallise my thoughts I replied that about £120 would be its worth.

"Twenty-five pounds then. I'll cure it for that."

"£25!" This was at a time when a farm worker's weekly wage was less than that figure. Twenty-five pounds was a lot of money. Did the old boy think I was that much of a mug that I would part with £25 for some gypsy's charm?

"You give me £25 now and the cow will be walking before I leave, you'll see."

"If you can cure it so that it walks up and down that meadow without limping then I might give you £25," I offered.

"No Mister, I want my money first. I'm not saying you look like a twister, but I been caught before by farmers. I've cured their horses and cattle and they won't pay up."

"If I were to pay you now what's to stop you making off? If the vet can't find out what's wrong I'm sure you can't." I thought the small fellow would turn and go at this rebuff. Instead he continued to argue while I turned more to ridicule. While this was going on the postman appeared in the yard, his presence spotted by the gypsy type.

"Does your postman call every day? If you can trust him you give him the £25 to hold. I'll cure your beast now and come back tomorrow morning when the postman calls to collect my money from him. You can't be twisted that way."

There seemed nothing wrong with this proposal. I couldn't see how I could lose and I know our postman to be as honest as they come. So I agreed if the postman was willing to be banker. He seemed a little amazed by the request, as well he might, but did not object. I duly fetched £25 and entrusted it to the postman, who wrote me a receipt on the back of an envelope from the Inland Revenue.

When accompanying the gypsy man back to the loose box he refused to do whatever he was going to do unless he was left on his own.

He did not want anyone 'knowing the secret.' As he insisted, I left him alone and then had time to wonder what sort of a fool I must be to engage in this ridiculous exercise. The gypsy man must have been with Annabel a good twenty minutes and it began to worry me that he might be doing something harmful to the cow; yet no bovine protest could be heard. When he eventually emerged he simply said: "Tis done Mister. I'll be back in the morning," walked straight to his vehicle and drove away. My first thought was that he would not appear tomorrow, knowing he had fed me a load of rubbish – and the more fool me to go along with this pantomime. Back to the loose box where Annabel was still lying down in exactly the same position as when the gypsy arrived. I didn't even bother to try and get her to stand. When returning to the house Clive emerged from the dairy door: "Did you see that little lorry thing here a little while ago?" he asked.

"Not to worry. Just a didicoy after scrap," I fibbed.

About a half hour later, while in black mood examining the bills that had arrived with the post, there came a knocking at the door and Clive stuck his head into the kitchen: "She's up! Annabel's standing okay. Reckon McTeggert was right: that was shock and she's taken time to get over it." All that issued in response to Clive's excitement was a murmured "Oh". In haste to get to the loose box I even overlooked changing slippers for Wellingtons. True to Clive's words, Annabel was standing, happily chewing the cud.

"Let's turn her out into the meadow and see how she goes," I suggested. Clive opened the gates and out the cow walked. I watched as Clive drove her up the meadow. Missing the calf she returned on her own at a trot. No sign of lameness; no sign of pain or tenderness. Extraordinary. More than that, it was incredible.

We had Annabel out of the loose box twice more that day and again early the next morning. She could not have been more nimble. Our postman usually arrived about nine and the moment he pedalled into the yard the gypsy man's vehicle chugged in behind him. He must have been lying in wait. The man's first words were: "Can I have my money, Mister." He didn't even ask if the cow was up and running; nor did he go and see. I told the postman to hand over the cash and intended to try and learn more of the gypsy's obvious skills. No sooner was the money in his hand and counted than he was back in his vehicle and away, with no more than a parting: "She'll milk well for you, Mister."

Later that week McTeggert dropped by. He had come to take another look at Annabel and was pleased to hear she was up and walking. Obviously it had been shock but he admitted to never coming across a case quite like this before. It did not seem wise to mention the little gypsy man – professional jealousy and all that. Additionally, on much reflection, I had come to think I was the victim and the gypsy the beneficiary of extraordinary coincidence. The rational explanation for the lameness must be shock.

It was probably about a couple of weeks later that I was again confronted by the Romany woman and her basket of lucky heather, "Hello," I said, "what brings you back again?"

"You'll need to seal the charm now that your cow is cured." She held out a sprig of white heather.

I checked myself from telling her I didn't want to hear any more of that rubbish and to be off, but countered with: "How do you know the cow is still well?"

"He never fails if he says it can be done. You'll have to seal the charm if you want the cow to stay well." The sprig of white heather was still held out before me.

"I've already bought one of those for a shilling. Surely that's enough".

"That was different. This one is for the cure. It is yours for five shillings and the cow will keep well. If you don't buy, the cow will be no good."

"Five shillings," I exploded. "What sort of fool do you think I am. You can keep your charm, thank you!"

There was a wild look in those dark eyes as she countered with: "You'll be a fool if you waste the charm." With that she turned and walked away. Perhaps she expected me to call her back, who knows, but my annoyance was such that I wanted no more of this nonsense. Even so, to be honest, a more than usual interest was taken in Annabel's welfare during the following weeks. The lameness did not recur and she milked well. So much for gypsy magic. So much so until later that summer.

Clive was concerned: "You better get McTeggert to see if there is anything wrong. The Cow's Best Friend has been to Annabel three times and she still hasn't taken." The Cow's Best Friend was the name used for the Milk Marketing Board's artificial inseminator – behind his back, of course. Annabel had failed to 'take' – become pregnant - after three visits. So I sent for the vet. McTeggert came, whisky breath and all. Poked, felt and asked questions. While answering, a dread thought occurred; the gypsy's charm. It was not mentioned to McTeggert.

After more failed attempts by the Cow's Best Friend to impregnate Annabel and more visits and conjecture by McTeggert, I decided at last to casually mention the business with the gypsy – although not the fact that I had paid him £25. I didn't want the vet to up his charges feeling I had money to chuck away. He listened patiently and did not engage in ridicule. "Some of these Romany people have osteopathic skills. Your man may have helped, but there's no relation between lameness and this business. What you're seeing now is the result of delayed shock."

We never did get Annabel in calf and, sadly, she had to be fattened and sent to market. Without telling why, I asked around fellow farmers if any knew where a wild-eyed gypsy woman selling lucky heather could be found or a little didicoy type in a pick-up made from an old Ford van. Some had seen them but none knew where they could be found. I would have dearly liked to talk with both, if only to convince myself the experience with Annabel was all a lot of hocus-pocus. As fate decreed, I never set eyes on those characters again.

It causes my wife some amusement that I now never turn away a gypsy selling lucky heather without a purchase. Fortunately they are rarely encountered these days.

Football Progress

For many sport is an absorbing interest, and for some an obsession. It appears that the majority of the British population either participate or follow sport in one or more of its diverse forms. I am one of that minority who find little attraction in these activities, believing that there are more enjoyable and fruitful ways of occupying one's leisure time on this earth. To my shame I confess to only once having attended a football match as a spectator, and then because a friend was a member of the team and had induced in me a feeling of guilt if I did not support the local club's 'great day'.

Most villages in these parts have football teams, varying from the decidedly casual to the aspiring imitators of professionals. That for whom my friend played was in the latter category yet has, as far as I am aware, the distinction of never having won the district league championship cup in more than seventy football seasons. However, they did reach the final at least twice, one being in 1947 – or was it '48? – the occasion when I was persuaded to be a spectator.

In its formative years the club had chosen black shorts and orange shirts as colours, later discovering that this was more or less the same uniform identifying players of Wolverhampton Wanderers, the famous national team. Thus our local team decided to use Wanderers as a suffix title, presumably as an act of appreciation; or perhaps anticipation. In view of the club's subsequent performance

Wolverhampton Wanderers would hardly be flattered by the former, although possibly amused.

The team manager and self-appointed trainer for many years during my youth was Eddie Burbridge, the village schoolmaster, a man of high ideals and much energy, if somewhat hindered by the continual steaming up of his glasses on the field and the poor material from which he sought to fashion capable players. The labourers and artisans were keen enough, if lacking the aptitude that would transform them into masters of the ball. The Wanderers did occasionally win their matches, although in most seasons they ended up near or at the bottom of the league table. Thus there was great excitement when the team actually reached the final of the 1947 – or 1948 – season. Their opponents were the Longham Lads, a team also not particularly renowned for their prowess on the pitch, so if Lady Luck smiled on the Wanderers this really might be their big day. Sadly, this proved to be one of those occasions when Lady Luck was conspicuous by her absence.

There had been a period of spring drought and those supporters who had prepared the home pitch on the Friday evening before the great event were well satisfied with the conditions of the field, laboriously mown with the club's spluttering motor mower, which burned so much oil and discharged so much blue smoke that two rounds of the area was about all an operator could take before having to be relieved.

An audience to this activity was a bunch of Billy Hastings' heifers on the adjoining over-grazed meadow. They stood in a line along the sagging barbed wire fence, doleful eyed and with the occasional mooed salutation. Alas, it was not the grass cutters and white liners that were the attraction, rather the smell of new mown grass, the first of the season, which remained long after the lawn mower fumes had wafted away. This was far too tempting and that night the animals broke out, a none too difficult job as Billy Hastings was never one to look to his fences until they were breached.

The short-trimmed pitch may not have afforded any feed, but the lush herbage surrounding it certainly did. The hoof parade to and fro across the pitch did little damage, although a substantial amount of excreta was deposited. Much worse was the decision of one bovine, as bovines will, to seek a beneficial body-rubbing against one of the south end goal posts. At a guess the posts had stood since the Wanderers were formed and wood rot had set in, as the itching heifer discovered after just two or three rubs. The animal was so startled when the post snapped and the cross bar came down that it bolted into the net and, thus enveloped, took off in fright straight through the leafy hawthorn hedge behind. Unable to free itself from the net and driven by panic, the heifer careered through a shrubbery, a garden and then another hedge on to the road. This probably occurred near dawn, for a Mrs Carrington, who had risen to let her mewing cat, out was very surprised to see what she took to be a cow festooned with leaves, twigs and even the odd daffodil trot past her front gate. Being recently removed from Chelsea and innocent of rural matters, she concluded the decorated beast was an old village custom connected with the coming May Day festival.

The next to encounter the errant heifer was the postman, who being a Wanderer supporter, was quick to see the foundation garment for the animal's leafy array was a goal net from the playing field. He made haste to the red 'phone box on the corner of Friar's Lane to alert Eddie Burbridge: "I hope you'll refund the twopence I just used to ring you Eddie, but I thought you ought to know I just seen what look like one of Billy Hastings' cows goin' up Friar's Lane wearing' one of your goal nets."

Eddie Burbridge's glasses steamed up twice as fast as usual when he reached the playing field and beheld the devastation. Mustering his helpers, he took frantic measures to find and erect a new goal post and secure a net from another local team that was playing away. An attempt to remove the numerous bovine deposits was none too successful due to their decidedly fluid nature. Scraping up with shovels appeared to have spread the offending material around even more. By much diligent effort some sort of order was restored to the pitch to enable the referee to blow his whistle promptly on time at 2 o'clock for the kick-off.

There must have been a good two hundred spectators if not more, a record crowd for a special occasion as home matches normally never drew above fifty. Young males predominated, with the odd knot of girls and women.

It was soon apparent that sections of the crowd were there

more for the pleasure of shouting mild abuse at the players than for appreciation of the finer points of soccer. A familiar voice was among them.

"I didn't know you were a football fan, Nasty?", I shouted during a lull in the din.

"There's a lot you don't know. I often come to cheer the home side on."

After a while I noticed that Nasty's words were directed at both teams and there was very little cheer in these utterances. He clearly came for the pleasure of reviling the players knowing that he could do this without the risk of a punch on the nose. In those days the stoic behaviour of players towards the spectators was the accepted norm. A supporter might holler at the unfortunate who missed a goal: "A one-legged man in a bum kicking contest would do better than you," and the player involved would not exhibit the slightest reaction to such a taunt.

Most of the first half of the game was without major incident and no goals were scored. Eddie Burbridge, playing inside right, managed to kick one of his own men in the ankle when aiming for the ball, no doubt because his glasses were steamed up. To the unfortunate victim's credit he stuck it out to the end although hobbling around to no purpose for most of the time. Inevitably Billy Hastings' heifers' contributions to the pitch did have an effect, although not in the way one might expect for I saw no one slip. A rolling stone may gather no moss; a rolling football most certainly gathers that which is messy, as evidenced by the fact that when kicked hard a spray of the substance adhering fanned out over those close by. It was not long before the white and lemon colours of the Longham Lads developed a decidedly khaki sheen, and while less obvious on the Wanderers' garb, most players had developed freckled faces. Occasionally some of the flotsam reached the edges of the crowd. Poodle Diggins, whose poor eyesight had led him to take up a position by the centre line, pushed past me a half hour into the game. "Going already, Mr Diggins?"

"I didn't come here to be crapped on," he grunted.

Just before half-time the Wanderers made a determined effort to score. Their centre forward was an exceptionally tall lad, about six feet five, whose name I never learned or have forgotten. He was another schoolmaster whom Eddie Burbridge had imported from Ipswich earlier in the season, the attraction being the fellow's long legs which, as I observed on this occasion, enabled him to outrun everyone else on the field. His expertise with the ball, or rather lack of it , was the problem, and even a novice like myself could recognise a great deal of foot fumbling which brought him much unkind comment from the more raucous element in the crowd. His stature was such that the club obviously had difficulty in fitting him out in Wanderers colours. Both shirt and shorts were far too small despite the generous cut of such garments in those days.

During the spurt of activity near half-time some nifty passing by two of the Wanderers' backs put the ball with the tall centre forward, and away up the field he went towards the Longham Lads' goal, to the accompaniment of much cheering and excitement. With the opposition's defence spread there was a good chance of scoring. Watching him from the Wanderers' goal end I suddenly became aware of a white area above the centre forward's black shorts. Unable to take the strain of this extra effort, the securing element of the shorts had failed and was exposing his buttocks under the too short-orange shirt.

Judging by the delighted screams from a group of girls near the Longham Lads goal end this was not all that was exposed before the poor fellow abandoned his run and retrieved the shorts that had descended to his knees. There was, as was to be expected, a chorus of ribald shouts from the more uncouth members of the crowd, above all the strident voice of Nasty yelling: "What you got holdin' them up? Some owd gal's knicker elastic?" This episode was more in keeping with one of those *Carry On* film farces, only at this time they were still in the future.

The poor centre forward hurriedly left the field and did not return until after the half-time break. The security of the black shorts – if they were the same pair – was now reinforced with a white belt. Sadly the incident had given the barrackers in the crowd a prize excuse for aiming insults at the unfortunate man, who resumed his position on the field to a chorus of chants such as: "Knicker elastic; he's fantastic." Clearly the poor fellow was weighed down with embarrassment and unable to cope with the barrage of cheap jibes. In a supreme effort to redeem himself he scored in less than a minute after play was resumed. The only problem was that the ball went into the Wanderers' net. The cat calls had obviously caused disorientation with the practice of teams changing ends at half time.

There were no more goals and while Longham Lads never scored they won the league cup that year. As for the Wanderers' centre forward, he resigned from the club and – I have it on good authority – forsook football for yoga and meditation. Whatever his achievements in life, one thing is certain, and that is his lasting fame in these parts, where middle-aged locals regularly entertain or bore pub customers with the tale of how Knicker Elastic scored an own-goal in a long-gone league championship.

In truth my sole visit to a soccer match was definitely entertaining. While that occasion turned into a comedy act, it should not detract from the enjoyment of players and followers who regularly participate or support this popular sport. I have never ventured near another match but I am told many things have changed since the late nineteen-forties.

About forty years on, the Wanderers again reached the district league final, the 1988 season - or was it '89? Of course, none of those who played in the match I witnessed are still active in the Wanderers, who now have a nice new clubhouse and changing rooms as an annexe to the village hall. One of the developments over the intervening years has been the much higher profile afforded village clubs by the local press; which really hasn't much else to stick between the mass of adverts on its pages. Before the more recent final, a press reporter and photographer descended on the club by appointment to gather material for a feature, which was duly published in the week preceding the match date. Fifteen smiling faces of players and officials posed around the steps of the clubhouse door was the leading photograph to the article. The team were unaware and the newspaper staff did not notice that some prankster had substituted a K for the stick-on letter D in the word Wanderers above the clubhouse door as well as removing an E and an R completely. All much to the delight of the successors of the likes of Nasty, and since then the distorted sobriquet has come into brazen and regular use. Alas, there is, by all account, even less social decorum at a football match these days.

An account of the recent final in which the Wanderers participated was given me by old Rue, long retired from the farm but no less agile in body and mind. A few days after the match, which the Wanderers lost six-three, I stopped by Rue's cottage to have a word, having seen him hoeing in the garden.

"Didn't see you at the football match last Saturday," he remarked.

"Haven't been to one since I was about 17 or 18," I answered. "Never been really interested."

"Use to go a lot when I were young. Ain't been for years until last Saturday. When I was a workin' I'd rather spend me Saturday afternoons with me 'taters and sprouts. No time for standin' about hollerin' at a lot of idiots tryin' to kick a ball into a net. I'd have done better than to have gone last Saturday the way they carry on nowadays. Somethin' terrible: enough to make owd Eddie Burbridge turn over in his grave if that's where he be – that'd certainly make his owd glasses steam up completely the way they carry on now." Rue extracted his tobacco tin from his hip pocket as he spoke and proceeded to roll a fag.

"What's changed? The way they play the game?" I queried.

"Game!" was the indignant response. "Game you call it. Thas like a bloody circus now. Only went 'cause Charlie Hepplewhite said I oughter to support the home team and offered to take me in his little owd plastic three-wheeler. Blast man, you should have heard the row when we got there. A loud speaker a blarin' out that bloody row what pass for music nowadays. And you should have seen what was prancin' up and down the pitch. Half a dozen young gals in next to nothin' with their lallies pushed up and out by the little bit they were wearin' up top and their rear ends stuck out just as bad. Each bangin' on a little drum and one of 'em out in front a twistin' and twirlin' a stick. All proper disgustin' and I don't know how their mothers and fathers let 'em do it."

"Drum majorettes," I explained. "Anyway I thought you had an eye for the niceties of what the Good Lord gave women."

"There's a time and place for everything, and you ain't a goin' to tell me a bunch of young gals a struttin' up and down like that and excitin' young fellars has got anything to do with football. Might be all right in front of a knockin' shop but not on our playin' field; thas my opinion."

There was no opportunity to interject before Rue vehemently continued to impose his views: "And that ain't all, the way the players carry on these days is a disgrace. They argue with the ref', they shouts back at the crowd and makes rude signs; but you should see what happen when one of them scores a goal. Blast man, they run around huggin' and kissin' each other or jumpin' on each others backs like a pair of dogs matin'; proper disgustin'. Mind you, some of them players has got such long hair they might be women for all I knows. When I was a lad they'd have been locked up for some of the things that were goin' on there Saturday. No, you won't get me a goin' to anything like that again. I'm stickin' with me 'taters and sprouts on a Saturday afternoon."

Somehow, Rue with his well-known interest in reproduction and associated matters did not come over convincingly as the offended moralist. I feel the real reason for his displeasure was the passing of the ordered, stiff-upper-lip behaviour to be seen on the soccer field in his young days. Village veterans find it hard to accept change, and I admit to sympathising with Rue's parting assessment on this occasion to the effect that the Wanderers are indeed a collection of their new uncouth nickname.

Near One For Nasty

It was accepted that Nasty was a rogue and a petty thief; what annoyed us all was that he never really got caught out. Every community has its bad lot, and we suffered Nasty. While many people would have been delighted to see him apprehended by the law and had few qualms about shopping him, Nasty was always the fish that slipped off the hook. That said, he had some anxious moments, and those of us who knew his artful ways never hesitated to make him sweat if an opportunity arose. His villainy was too well known for most locals to be taken in, but it was a different matter with newcomers faced with his cheery smile and generous promises. Many were the gullible who continued to think of him as 'that nice helpful man'.

One who once uttered these sentiments was the wife of a serviceman who had evacuated herself and three children from Wimbledon in the early days of 'the war', and was resident in the village until her husband returned from overseas five years later. An exceedingly pretty woman who, like many so fortunate, was well aware of her standing in male eyes and had no qualms about putting it to advantage. To supplement the power of her looks she was extremely good at playing the poor little war wife whose husband was fighting for king and country. Not until after hostilities did we learn the absent husband had spent most of his service overseas in an administrative post on an air force training station in Rhodesia far from the enemy. Nevertheless, Mrs Brightby earned the sympathy of the village, who assumed the husband was flying combat and in constant peril. She and her family were recipients of many gifts and acts of kindness through this supposed situation which the lady did nothing to dispel.

I would not class Nasty as having been a ladies' man, but like most males he was susceptible to a pretty face. We knew he had been married at one time. His only comment when enquires were made about his former matrimonial status was: "I soon got rid of her. No man could live with the likes of her." From what others have said it was definitely the other way round. I have no knowledge of how Nasty became acquainted with Mrs Brightby, and can only recall that he boasted to other men on the farm of his good standing in her eyes for the various favours he had been able to do for her: "I'll be all right there, do you see," said with a knowing look and a grin. If Nasty was really under the impression that Mrs Brightby would reward him with amorous attention he was most certainly deluding himself. It was very evident that she considered herself to be on a much higher social plane than we genuine country folk, apart from the fact that she was ever the dutiful wife and mother and showed no interest in dances and social activities that were the stamping grounds of those servicemen's wives looking for a good time.

Nevertheless there were many males in the village on whom Mrs Brightby's good looks had effect, the Guv'nor being one of them. It was at breakfast one morning that I first became aware of this when he lowered his *Daily Mail* and in unnaturally casual tone instructed me to deliver a half hundredweight of potatoes to the woman. "She stopped and asked me where she could buy some as those in her garden were all worm eaten. Can't charge her, not with her husband away fighting, poor woman." The Guv'nor's wife, who knew well her husband's weakness before an attractive member of the fair sex, picked up a couple of dirty dishes and headed for the kitchen sink with the comment: "Vera Sparrow hasn't any in her garden this year. I expect she would like some too." The Guv'nor mumbled acknowledgement and retreated behind his newspaper; not quickly enough to hide his flushed face. The Guv'nor's wife gave me a triumphant smile. Vera Sparrow might have had a husband in the army overseas but she was fat, buck-toothed, and a role model for the proverbial 'face like the backside of a bus'. The garden of her council house hadn't seen a spade or fork since the day her husband was called up.

The only immediate method of delivering a half-hundredweight of spuds was to lift the sack into the large carrier on the front of the old trade bike we used around the farm for short journeys, and to push it the half mile to the Brightby's cottage. It would have been too unbalanced to attempt to ride. Thus this was not a task I accepted gracefully, particularly as there was a long incline on the way along the road. My mental cursing of the Guv'nor increased as I tired, for this was not an easy task for a lean sixteen year-old . When the Brightby's front gate was reached I was not in a very good mood. The front lawn was neatly mowed and I wondered whom she had conned into doing the task with a push mower. On the other hand, the kitchen garden remained nearly as neglected as Vera Sparrow's, for although Mrs Brightby had found someone to dig and plant a small area, the carrots, lettuce and other vegetables were choked with weeds. My intention was to dump the sack on the doorstep and depart, but Mrs Brightby had obviously heard the inordinate squeaking of the gate and was at the front door to meet me.

"This is kind of your father. Do thank him. Most generous. Could you carry the sack round to the back for me?"

I complied, although my thoughts were to the effect that it wouldn't hurt the recipient to take them round herself. Surely she could manage a half hundredweight that distance.

"In here please." She opened the back door and pointed towards a small alcove at the end of a short passage. I deposited the sack as bid. At that moment the kitchen door was opened by one of her offspring and a large white rabbit flopped out into the passage.

"Oh Justin; keep Snow White in the kitchen dear. You don't want her running outside." Another small child appeared and attempted to pull the rabbit back by an ear while Mrs Brightby gently assisted the animal's return with her foot.

"Keep the door closed." And turning to me: "They do love it so. I let them have it in the kitchen to play with. That nice man who works for your father gave it them. What is his name now?"

It was not a question of which 'nice man' in my mind, even though the Guv'nor employed five. "Nasty," I said and seeing Mrs. Brightby's pained and puzzled expression, continued: "He's called Nasty. Everyone calls him Nasty and he doesn't mind."

"How uncivilised," she scolded. "What is his real name?"

"Well, er, I don't remember. I think its Woodyard or Wood something. You see everyone calls him Nasty. I can ask my father if you really want to know."

"I suppose you country people don't know any better and think it funny. Well I don't. He has been very good to me. Went to a lot of trouble to select a nice tame rabbit for the children. I know it is old and one of his favourites and he didn't really want to part with it. He tells me the young ones he breeds are inclined to scratch if handled whereas Snow White is used to it and ideal for children and he sold it for a very reasonable price. I am certainly not going to call him . . . what you said."

"Oh," I said, making tracks for the gate. There wasn't much else it would have been prudent to say knowing that Nasty didn't keep tame rabbits, let alone breed them. Someone somewhere in this locality had probably lost a pet rabbit. Intrigued, I mounted the clumsy trade bike and pedalled off, not even waiting to respond to Mrs Brightby's parting request to convey her thanks to the Guv'nor.

Naturally, I took the first opportunity to tackle Nasty on the subject. He was in one of the stables harnessing a mare.

"Thought you said you didn't keep rabbits." It was an ill chosen approach, for Nasty's "I don't tell you everything" suggested he guessed he was about to be held to account.

"When Rue was thatching the wheat stacks on Wood Field and he was saying how he had a black doe that had a litter of ten, you said keeping rabbits was a waste of time." There was possibly a note of triumph in this assertion on my part, for it brought the guarded: "What I say and what I do is two different things!"

"Mrs Brightby says you gave her kids a white rabbit called Snow White. You told her it was your favourite and that you'd got others but they might scratch. Where do you keep all these rabbits?

I've never seen any hutches round the back of your house."

But Nasty was not to be drawn and all I got was a "You don't see everything" while the horse got a very tight girth belt as it was pulled up an extra notch due to the horseman's irritation. Not that Nasty was a horseman; he was only occasionally given the task of using one for tumbrel work when no one else was available.

Nasty was hardly a regular employee, more an irregular, since one rarely knew when he would turn up for work. The Guv'nor only employed him because at that time there was a dearth of farm labour and agriculture was then a very labour intensive industry. It was noticeable that when Nasty was on the farm I was frequently sent to work with him, the Guv'nor's thinking doubtless being that Nasty was more likely to contribute a liitle effort for his pay if the Guv'nor's son was on hand. Such was the case a few days later when a tumbrel load of sugar beet tops had to be transported to the cattle down on the off-farm. The tumbrel loaded, I lounged on the soft leaves as Nasty sat on the front of the tumbrel 'Get upping' and 'Go oning' to the horse with an occasional slap of the reins.

The sun beamed, and in my prostrate position I enjoyed my idleness. Then I realised the sun shouldn't have been causing me to shade my eyes if we were going to the off-farm.

"What are you going this way for?" I asked.

"Want to call at the shop and get some matches. That ain't much further this way."

The fact was that the way we were going would add another quarter mile to the journey, if not a bit more. Being quite happy to continue my own inactivity on the beet tops and waste the Guv'nor's time and money, I said no more. In any case it would not be me who was called to account if the Guv'nor questioned the selection of this circuitous route.

Then Nasty started to sing: only Nasty most certainly couldn't sing. The rendering was a popular tune called *Ice Cold Katie*. "Ice Cold Katie won't you marry the soldier . . ." discord at its best. A squeaking door could not have sounded less melodious. Puzzled as to why we – the mare and I – were so entertained I suddenly remembered that we would pass Mrs Brightby's cottage. Probably the real reason for Nasty coming this way. If he was deluding himself that Mrs. Brightby would be impressed by his torture of a catchy tune, so be it. Unkind as it probably was, I shouted: "You feeling ill, Nasty?" put my hands over my ears and lay back in the beet tops and enjoyed the unexpected autumn warmth.

The vocal mutilation evidently did not go unheard by the individual it was supposed to charm, because the row ceased abruptly and with a cheery "Whoa there!" the tumbrel came to a halt, followed by an even more cheery "Good Mornin' Mam".

Mrs. Brightby's response sounded far from cheerful: "I'm glad I caught you. Snow White – the rabbit – it belongs to someone else!"

There was a brief silence before an indignant "That can't do. That were one of mine."

I kept low in the beet tops as the concerned voice of Mrs. Brightby continued: "The children had their friends from Longham here - the ones who they go to kindergarten with - for a party. They lost their rabbit a few weeks ago. Found the cage door open one morning. When they saw Snow White they recognised it as theirs. No mistake because it has a small black mark on the right back paw. I've worked out that they lost theirs the same day as you brought me Snow White, it's not even called Snow White, its name is Charlie, its a he rabbit."

One has to acknowledge that when it came to the instant excuse Nasty was a master: "Well the morning I brought that rabbit to you that had got out and was runnin' around my garden. That had done that afore and I didn't think nothin' of it. If it ain't Snow White I can only think I picked up the wrong one. Where do you say your friends live?"

"Longham. Their name is Cottee. The house is two miles from here; must be. You are surely not going to tell me a rabbit travels two miles so quickly? And what happened to your rabbit ? It would have been around your garden and you would have seen it later? If this is a prank then it is very cruel. The children are heartbroken." There was growing anger in Mrs. Brightby's voice, countered by Nasty really trying to turn on the charm.

"If thas a buck that'd travel several miles in a day lookin' for a doe. Reckon that got drawn to my place and frightened Snow White away. Thought that were a bit difficult to catch. My fault. I should have looked at it better when I got hold of her and afore I put her back in the cage. Never you mind now, I'll have a nice tame rabbit for your young'uns tonight, I promise. I wouldn't have had anything happen like this for the world I wouldn't. Just you don't fret. I'll have you another rabbit this evenin'."

Because of the tumbrel's high sides Mrs Brightby may have been unaware of my presence and in the circumstances I thought it best if this remained the case. Doubt if she was taken in by Nasty's explanation even if placated with the promise of another pet rabbit that evening. The tumbrel eventually resumed its rumbling motion following an extra cheery "Never you mind. I'll bring you another rabbit tonight" from the driver. We rumbled on until I gauged we were out of earshot, then gleefully added to Nasty's discomfort.

"You better not let her down. You know who the Cottees are don't you? He's a police superintendent in Ipswich."

"Don't you start tellin' fibs boy. 'Sides I done nothin' wrong. I can't help it if I caught their rabbit by mistake."

"He is a police superintendent. You ask Wully when we get back to the farm." I pressed the point home. "I've seen the Cottee's rabbit hutches just inside their back gate. You can see them plainly when you bike along the Bergholt road".

"I ain't ever seen them," Nasty hissed.

He had seen them, all right. And it would have been easy enough to slip through the back garden gate at night and take a rabbit from the hutches.

"Where you going to get another one from by this evening? Got several more at home have you?" I chided, only to be firmly told: "Any more of your cheek and you'll be gettin' my hand across your lug hole you will." Not wanting to tempt providence, I said no more, at least until we had completed our duties and returned to the farm: "There's a white rabbit hopping across the Home Field" I shouted, sliding off the back of the tumbrel and then running off as fast as my legs would comply.

While Nasty may have deserved his name, my tormenting him as on this occasion does not say much for my own character. But Nasty was so cocky one never missed a chance to take him down a peg or two. Even if successful it had no lasting effect for he would soon bounce back again, as devious as ever. Naturally the business of Mrs Brightby's rabbit was related with much delight to other members of the farm staff. Nasty did keep his promisebut he did not turn up for work

on Saturday morning and he was extremely uncommunicative whenever I tried to raise the subject on the following Monday, usually being told to "Mind you're own bloody business". It was Clive, the cowman, who provided the answers. While drinking in the Anchor on Saturday evening he had encountered old Comey Smith, who informed him that the night before Nasty had arrived at his door asking to buy a white rabbit. Old Comey, who was well known for breeding rabbits for the table, didn't particularly want to part with any of his stock, turning down Nasty's offer. Nasty finally put down ten shillings, a not inconsiderable sum for a rabbit worth no more than two shilling and sixpence at best. Beggars cannot be choosers, and old Comey knew he must be confronted with a beggar: "Make it twelve and six and I'll think about it." So Mrs Brightby's children evidently got another rabbit. I guess only because Nasty feared that if he did not do something quickly the hand of the law might come his way. Undoubtedly the word superintendent was the real frightener for it must have been the only time Nasty parted with money for a rabbit – and a comparative fortune at that – which he could normally obtain by devious or dishonest means. At the time I really did think Mr Cottee was a police superintendent. Only later did I discover he was actually a superintendent in the fire service. Honestly.

Both Ends Bates

Sooner or later old Newson will appear in the farm yard for a mardle. I suppose conversation is one of the most popular pastimes for retired folk, although where Harry Newson is concerned the conversation usually developes into an exercise in nostalgia. There is certainly no one around here with a more encyclopaedic knowledge of people and events, and what he doesn't know or cannot recall is no obstacle to his relating a detailed account, imagination authoritatively filling the gaps.

On one occasion when he was regaling me with some involved account of who was related to some old girl who had recently popped off, he mentioned Arthur Bates. I had not heard that name for ages. In my mind it conjured up a very large bib-and-brace-overall-clad old fellow who used to work for Fenney the builder when I was a boy. He gave me the cigarette cards out of his Woodbine packets – or was it Players Weights he smoked? Whatever the brand, he gave me the cards, a charitable act which would never be forgotten by an avid collector of those colourful sets. I tried to visualise his face without success. Like so many individuals known and taken for granted, when departed one is unable to describe the countenance once so familiar.

"You ain't listenin' to what I'm sayin'," old Newson snorted.

"Sorry, I was just thinking about old Bates who worked for Fenney when I was a boy. Hadn't thought of him for years until you mentioned his name. Didn't they call him Both Ends? Not that I ever called him that. The other fellows did if I remember correctly. What happened to him?" "Churchyard these thirty years or more. Lot older than me was Arthur Bates. He'd be well over a hundred now if he were still a kickin'," old Newson mused, "Yes, Both Ends Bates. Thas goin' back a bit. Worked for Fenney and his father afore him. More than fifty year. Nice old fellow."

"Why did they call him Both Ends?" I had reservations as soon as the question was put: there was to be no retreat, for old Newson's face showed his delight.

"Yer mean to tell me you've been round here man and boy all your days and yer don't know about Both Ends Bates ? Do you sit yourself down on that bag of corn behind yer and I'll tell yer."

Old Newson was already seated on one of the paper sacks of seed wheat stacked in rows along the inner side of the barn wall, and his dog sat on the ground before him. Neither looked like being in any hurry to move. My thoughts were that I might as well hear whatever exaggerated tale he was going to spin in comfort, so I sat on the sack as instructed.

"Wasn't there some tale of him being attacked by a ferret when he was young?" I posed.

Harry Newson spread his legs and placed his stick between them before leaning forward on it, a stance frequently adopted when a monologue was in the offing.

"Well, that were the time Fenney's men – thas the old father, not the son that used to hang around Edie Mortlake – time they was doin' up the Lamb Farm House. That had been proper neglected and stood empty for years. I'm talkin' afore the Great War when I was a young whippersnapper meself and I reckon as how you weren't even a naughty thought in your father's head." I laughed dutifully.

"Now Bates bein' a weighty fellar were never one for standin' up if he could be sittin'. A good carpenter, a dab hand with a tenon saw, but he didn't use his owd legs more than he could help. That happened one nippy winter's day with a good sharp frost. Seems how Batesey had been swillin' too much beer, but instead of just going round the back wall of the house he makes for an old privy that stood under an ivy-hung hawthorn in the garden. Hadn't been used for years I doubt.

Anyways, Bates not bein' a standin' man he drops his trousers and sits down. All of a sudden the other men hears a scream the likes of what you've never heard. They run out of the house in time to see the privy door flung open and Bates shoot out, his trousers round his ankles and a damn grut ferret a swingin' back and forth between his legs."

"Ouch," I winced.

" 'Get it off' he cries, 'Get it off '." Well, the other fellows they rush and try to get the ferret off. Could they hell. You knows what an owd ferret is like when that get its teeth into anything, that ain't goin' to let go. In the end that took two fellows to force its jaws open. Poor old Bates he passed out and they had to get him to the Doc's. Put him in the builder's cart with the woodshavings and wheeled him there, they did. Thas an ill wind that somebody don't blow good, or whatever they say, 'cause the ferret turned out to be one of Billy Fogget's he'd lost a month afore. Expect the ferret found the old privy pail full of leaves a nice snug place to curl up in out of the cold. Well, there's that owd ferret a dreamin' away when suddenly the heavens open up on it. Short tempered things ferrets if they gets upset . . . well, stands to reason that one goes for the first thing he sees – and Bates was a big fellow."

I was ready to ask the obvious question. There was no need, for after the usual dab at his mouth with his handkerchief the narrator pressed on.

" 'Course he was holed."

"Holed?"

"Well, them ferret's teeth is pretty sharp. I once stood alongside Both Ends in the Gents at the Lamb and he was a sprayin' all over the place, just like the rose on the end of an owd watercan spout. Now would I tell yer a lie?" He had obviously caught the look of amused disbelief that I was unable to control, but then immediately assailed me with:

"What about his kids then ? That'll convince yer."

"Never knew he had any family. What do you mean?"

"He had two lots of twins, only the first was really triplets. One died. That shows yer he was holed."

The temptation to dismiss this with ridicule was resisted. Instead I parried with: "But you still haven't explained why he was known as Both Ends."

"You ain't give me a chance. I'm comin' to that. Well, a few years later, I think it were '21; that were one of the coldest winters I've known. Ground frozen solid and plenty of snow. Fenney's men couldn't work outside so they was in the workshop knockin' up coffins on spec' for Charlie Gaybarrow and doin' various other jobs. Now you remember what Fenney's place was like? That were near where you live."

"Yes, there was a long shed, end on to the road, where they stored all the wood and planking. At the other end was the workshop, tacked on like the bar of a T."

"But do yer remember what was in the workshop?" old Newson asked impatiently.

"There was one narrow bench along the far wall where they kept the tools and fixings, a wide bench in the centre where they did the work. Don't remember anything else. Oh yes, there was a little cast iron stove and a chimney against the other wall." I could visualise the workshop in my mind's eye, the heaps of sawdust and wood chips everywhere and the distinctive smell, a mixture of sawn deal and glue . . . for a moment childhood memories took hold, only to be banished by old Newson tapping me on the knee with his stick.

"That's it, young master: that little stove. Now Fenney – I'm talking about the old man – wouldn't let his men light it 'cause he was too worried the place would catch light with all that sawdust and wood shavings about, so he got a couple of them big paraffin burnin' Valor safety stoves to use in the shop when it were damp or cold. But one day in that hard winter it were so cold the fellows couldn't hardly feel their fingers so he gave permission for them to light up the cast iron stove provided they kept four buckets of water close by. The joiners were doin' some delicate job and yer can't work with cold fingers, can yer? Anyways, half way through the mornin' Arthur Bates comes in. He'd been puttin' up some shelves in the vicarage. He'd had to walk a half mile through a foot of snow – weren't no salting of the roads in them days – and he were out of puff by the time he got back to the workshop. Well, he takes his overcoat off and there's some chit-chat with the others when suddenly Bates gives out the almighty scream and jumps a good three feet in the air, so they said. What he done was sit down on top of the little cast iron stove, darn fool. He'd sat there afore 'cause that were never lit. Didn't realise until he felt the heat but then it were too late as his grut owd weight was on the way down. The stove were near red hot and his trousers caught fire. The other fellows dowsed the flames and put him face down in the builders cart and had a right owd job pushin' him up to the Doc's with all the snow about. The owd Doc he peeled off Bates' trousers and did he get a shock. He want to know what had been goin' on 'cause the burn marks on Bates' rear end spelt A TWOT. Honest to God. Yer see the stokin' plate on top of the stove were slightly curved and that had Black & Sons, Stowting, Kent cast on it, sort of standing out; don't know what they call it."

"Relief," I offered.

Old Newson gave me a puzzled look: "Shouldn't think he felt like relievin' himself for weeks. Anyways, as I was sayin' thas what he had on his bum - A Twot."

"Pull the other one," I protested.

He gave a contemptuous chuck of the head and fixed me with that supposedly stern look which I knew from experience held mischievous intent.

"And you supposed to be a thinkin' man and here am I havin' to explain a simple thing what should bo obvious to yer even if you'd just had a couple of glasses of me mushroom wine. Now just you think. On the first line that had Black and Sons but Bates only just touched the lid afore his retro-rockets took hold – yer see I keeps up with all this here space high jinks – so only the A in Black what was the highest letter on the curve of the lid caught him. Most of his weight went on the next line and he picked up TOWT out of Stowting, only being back-to-front that read TWOT . Good job there weren't a third line or he'd a got that on his dilberries!" There was a burst of mirth followed by the usual dabbing of lips with the red spotted handkerchief.

"That has to be the most ridiculous story I've heard for a long while", was my comment on standing up.

Old Newson feigned a hurt look: "You thinks what yer likes but thas true, 'cause I seen it with my own eyes, plain as could be, A TWOT. Ask Rue Scrutts, he'll tell yer it's true. Batesey earned many a free pint in the Lamb by droppin' his trousers to show his scars. He was on to a good thing until one evening when Mrs Aidswell was a collectin' for the Red Cross. First thing she saw when she opened the Tap Room door was Batesey's backside with 'A TWOT' starin' her in the face. Someone had just offered him a pint for a quick flash. That cost the landlord a couple of brandies to bring her round and he banned Bates from then on. Well I mean, a God fearin' woman like her might have had a heart attack seein' somethin' like that. As it was they say she had nightmares for years about that great big bum . . ."

"But you still haven't told me why Bates was called Both Ends," I cut in, sensing old Newson was about to embark on a survey of other people's nightmares which would have meant another ten-minute monologue.

"Ain't I just told yer? Didn't he get into trouble both ends – his front end and his rear end? You just ain't thinkin' today are yer. Same trouble as Batesey?"

"How's that?"

"Well, his trouble was he didn't think to look where he was goin' to sit. Nor did you when you sat on that sack, otherwise you'd have seen there were a bird dropping."

Hurry Hadstock

The number of agricultural holdings in this parish is only a fraction of what it was a half century ago; as it is in just about every parish in the country I should think. The small places have gone and the surviving farms have all grown in the number of acres. By my count we once had eight farming neighbours of whom just two remain.

One holding that has disappeared – or to be more accurate has become part of a small empire raised by an agribusinessman in the adjacent parish – is that worked for a good thirty years by Harry Hadstock. In his day Hadstock was the most progressive farmer around here, insomuch as he quickly embraced the newest ideas and equipment. With hindsight I think he was an exceptionally restless soul who always had to be up and doing. Indeed, Hadstock was characterised by his desire to literally be first in the field, for I cannot recall an occasion when he was not the first to sow and the first to harvest, albeit that this was often far too early, the consequences of which were that he was frequently the last to finish. A prime example was the year he sowed spring barley at the end of January only to have both tractor and seed drill stuck fast up to their axles in a wet patch on the second pass down the field. The tractor was eventually retrieved after a twenty-four hour muddy struggle, but the drill remained bogged down for a month.

It was Harry Hadstock's haste that caused some local wit to dub him Hurry Hadstock and thus this appropriate manipulation of his Christian name caught on. Moreover, he came to be called Hurry to his face by all and sundry, apparently accepting this without offence. Perhaps he thought this was how people believed he favoured the pronunciation of his name due to the fact that in his wife's strong Scots accent he was always 'Hurry'. Nora Hadstock was a handsome and intelligent woman, the daughter of one of the many migrant farmers from the Borders who came to East Anglia between the two wars. I've heard more than one village prude express the opinion as to how 'the likes of her should get herself married to the likes of him'. Very much a loner, she appeared quite content with her own company in that great ugly red brick farmhouse that some frugal Victorian had raised. While both Hurry and Nora Hadstock were of amiable nature, they did not socialise with the rest of the farming fraternity or participate in village activities. Hurry's sole interest appeared to be his farm, and if his wife had any interest outside domesticity it was unknown to the gossips who often pondered on what she found to do in that large house all day. However, it was known that she was an avid reader, regularly collecting several volumes of fiction from the mobile library. The Hadstocks had no children. Our Rue, whose favourite topic was procreation and attendant matters, proclaimed: "The trouble be that either she's got no apples in the apple room or Hurry is always in too much of a hurry." He further qualified the last assertion with more graphic detail and in the unnecessarily crude terms that is his way. It never seems to have occurred to Rue, or others similarly vociferous, that the Hadstock's may not have wanted children.

Hurry's impatience was well known, as was his frugality in some matters. At a time when the average number of farm workers per hundred acres was three, he ran his 120 acres with one man, Peter Bone, a cousin of our cowman's wife, a few years younger than Hurry but imbued with the same insatiable urge to complete tasks as quickly as possible. A commendable objective, but the standard of work achieved usually left much to be desired; the old adage, more haste less speed, was often valid on Hadstock's farm. Farmer and employee were well suited, for I doubt if a more leisurely inclined worker would have tolerated Hurry for long.

There was, however, a noticeable difference between the two in that despite their mutual haste, Peter Bone never came to any harm, whereas Hurry was extraordinarily accident prone. I can recall him with a bandaged foot, the result of trying to read the time on the church clock while consolidating hard-core with a hand rammer. Additionally, he twice had an arm in a sling for some weeks, and on another occasion a large sticking plaster on his chin and cheek, the causes of all being unknown to me. If his person suffered through his unguarded haste, his and others' property did more so. Once, when bound on some urgent business to town and preparing to exit from his farmyard, Hurry reversed at high speed into a plough he had forgotten was there. The robust plough was little harmed but Hurry's Ford 8 van was left with an ungainly shaped rear end and doors that could not be opened. Then there was the memorable occasion when Hurry was driving a tractor towing a cultivator along Frog Lane and without stopping pulled on to the verge to give an approaching bus more room to pass. The cultivator snagged the new chain link fence that Mrs Ludington-Witt had recently erected in front of her kitchen garden. Not until in the field, when looking back to see what sort of a tilth the cultivator was making, did Hurry become aware the implement was trailing fifty yards of chain link fencing with stakes attached. Hurry's haste also led to at least two Court appearances for speeding in built-up areas.

The local newspaper reported one case where the Chairman of the Bench was not impressed by the plea: "I had to get home quick 'cause I remembered I forgot to turn the light off in the meal shed and that were costin' me a fortune."

In the summer of 1949 word was that Hurry Hadstock had bought a combine harvester, a self-propelled model at that. Hitherto a large acreage farm at Bergholt was the only one in this district with a combine. Many farmers had not yet accepted that these machines had come to stay and the hard graft of pitching sheaves was on the way out. I overheard the Guv'nor and Billy Hastings complaining that Hadstock must have more money than sense, all right for dry places like Canada, not here. If the truth were known there was more than a touch of envy and a feeling of being upstaged. Even so, they were not far wrong in professing failure; not that it was the fault of the machine. Long before Hadstock's crop of winter barley was truly fit for combining the bright red Massey Harris was in action, Hurry's impatience getting the better of him. The combine roared and thumped its way up the field and back again but on the next run Peter Bone was encouraged to drive faster with the result that the machine became clogged. Furious activity ensued with Hurry opening the hatch above the straw walkers, then disappearing inside to cut and pull out the unripe straw wrapped round the beater. Having cleared the blockage Hurry raised his head out of the hatch and shouted to Bone to start up and run the threshing mechanism. Hurry was still standing on the straw walkers and did not anticipate their action was as violent as it proved to be when Bone let in the clutch. Instead of hoisting his feet out of the hatch as planned, Hurry lost his balance and slipped back onto the straw walkers. After any blockage a combine emits the blackest cloud of dust when first brought to life again. Hurry was tossed up and down on the straw walkers, deluged in dust, and finally ejected out of the back, cut, bruised and winded. Bone, assuming Hurry was walking behind, set off down the field. Coming back, as he later related: "I see a black fellow havin' a nap in the straw – but I thought that were strange 'cause you don't see many of them this way."

It took a lot of soap and hot water plus plasters to get Hurry back into reasonable shape. The bruises were so numerous he was more dalmatian than human. Nora Hadstock, no doubt mindful of the number of occasions her husband had injured himself, was concerned for the future if this trend continued and tried unsuccessfully to encourage Hurry to take out personal insurance. When this continued to be viewed as an unnecessary extravagance by Hurry, she secretly contacted an insurance salesman, hoping he could persuade her breadwinner to take this financial protection. Obviously she was wise enough not to mention his track record.

To a successful young life insurance agent a strong, fit, 39-year-old farmer with no history of illness sounded a good bet. It was a warm October day when he drove into Hadstock's farmyard bent on his mission of signing up the owner. On the stubble field beyond the buildings a tractor and high sided trailer was in the process of tipping something. The insurance man approached the tractor driver:

"My hat, something really pongs round here."

Peter Bone motioned towards the trailer: "Pig slurry."

"Oh well, rather your pig of a job than mine," the insurance man chortled. "Where is Mr. Hadstock?"

"Back of the trailer," Bone advised.

Hurry was trying to pry the bottom of the trailer back door open with a small crowbar without much success. For some reason the door was jamming. Hurry gave it a vicious thump with the crowbar and suddenly it swung free, three tons of slurry cascading out.

The insurance man was in the process of walking towards the rear of the trailer and retreated as the slurry flowed back towards him. He then saw a large blob of slurry rise from the mass and form a human-like shape. The insurance man wisely decided to continue his retreat, feeling this was not an opportune moment to engage the subject of his visit in discussing the merits of personal insurance.

Even after being hosed down and taking two hot baths, Hurry still retained a distinctive aroma. He was confined to sleeping on a camp bed in the outhouse for three nights and took several more baths before Nora would have him back in the house.

A month passed before the insurance agent appeared again. Hurry and Peter Bone were replacing the holed corrugated iron sheeting on the cart lodge. Hurry was on the roof with hammer and nails, Bone on the ground passing up the replacement galvanised sheets.

Hurry heard a car drive into the farmyard and hastily stepped to the corner of the roof to see who it was. New galvanised iron sheets can be very slippery, particularly if one was in too much of a hurry to wipe the muck off one's boots before getting up on a roof. Perhaps if Hurry had moved more slowly and carefully he might have been able to stop when he wanted to. It was fortunate that the old wood water-butt had recently been replaced with a large rectangular metal tank and that it was reasonably full. No one had drawn water from it since the spring and green algae had spread across the surface in the recent warm weather.

"Mr. Hadstock about?", enquired the insurance man from the open window of his Vauxhall.

"Up on the roof," Bone responded.

The insurance man drove on a little round the side of the building to behold a dripping human form, liberally draped with green algae, in the process of extracting itself from a water tank. Without doubt an instant assessment of the odds motivated the insurance man to put his foot down, swing the car violently round in the yard and make off towards the road. His determination to escape was such that he scraped the side of the Vauxhall against the wall as he swung out of the gate onto the road, probably sufficient to lose his own no claims bonus. Needless to say, he never came back.

While the insurance man must have mentally congratulated himself on avoiding a bad bet, he would probably have come out on the right side if he had signed up Hurry, who actually managed to reach retirement age in one piece. In the 'sixties the Hadstocks sold up and moved to a 300-acre farm in north Norfolk. It was typical of the man to take on more work when most of his age would have been thinking of retiring. Peter Bone, who lived with a married sister while in our village, went with the Hadstocks. Of course, Hurry didn't retire when he got to 65 and still hadn't slowed down when he got to 73, as is evidenced by his demise. Rushing to get to Cromer before the bank closed he wasn't quite quick enough getting across an unmanned level crossing just as a train was due. He did finally get to Cromer; courtesy of the police, in three black plastic bags containing several small messy pieces. Too late for the bank, though.

Within a month of his funeral we heard that Nora Hadstock had married Peter Bone. I'm sure this arrangement gave our village gossips something to chew over, if nothing more than the fact that she had become Nora Bone.

Up the Doc's

They still say 'up the Doc's', just as the 'they' of yesteryear said 'up the Doc's', despite the fact that for most village people it is now a case of descent, the sparkling new surgery being down in the valley. The expression may not have changed but the doctors and the venue have. Today's surgery is shiny clean, all plastic and glass finish with bold wall posters about parts of the human anatomy and subjects one would have hardly dare broach with the doctor in the confidence of his consulting room in the old days. Now there is a posse of receptionists, dispensers, nurses and doctors to deal with the poorly, whereas in my youth it was very much a one man affair. Sebastian Gates practised as the village doctor for a good thirty years and was held in some reverence by parishioners, which can be put down to his assumed ability to kill or cure.

He lived in one of those exceedingly plain red brick houses of 19th century origin, part of which was utilised as a surgery. One entered by a heavy varnished door to be confronted by a square wood panelled waiting room which matched the exterior of the building in aesthetic qualities. A polished pine bench ran round the walls, only interrupted by the outside entrance door and that which led into the doctor's consulting room. The decor was spartan: not a picture hung from the walls and no magazines or other reading material were provided for those who waited. The solitary window had a brown roller blind and the single light bulb suspended from the centre of the ceiling wore a circular brown shade. In short it was so dismal that it was enough to make you feel ill if you didn't when you entered. I always contrasted it to the public bar at the Lamb which was of similar size with wall benches, yet cosy and bright, the complete antithesis of Gates' waiting room.

Those who went 'up the Doc's' sat and waited their turn to enter the consulting room. When your turn came you simply entered after the previous patient had made an exit. There was never any vocal command of "Next" from within the holy of holies, which made me wonder how the chain of events was initiated. This remained unknown due to my never having been the first to arrive for morning surgery. The consulting room was almost as frugally adorned as the waiting room, with little to cheer the ailing patient other than the Doctor. In contrast to his surroundings Gates was an amiable man, most certainly bestowed with the celebrated good bedside manner. There was, alas, an exception to this generally pleasant demeanour. Gates had an Irish wife, a striking, tall, red-haired woman; striking in both senses. She was possessed of a violent temper, evident through the outbursts one occasionally heard while sitting in the waiting room. The focus of these tantrums appeared to be her husband. One could rarely make out what the trouble was or what was being said, even though Mrs Gates would sometimes be screaming at the top of her voice. The tirade was often accompanied by door slamming and the occasional crash, as if something had been thrown; plus the heated response of Gates, although always at far lower modulation than his wife's outbursts. The result of such incidents was to leave the good doctor in a decidedly tetchy mood, thus removing his usual tolerance of the regular hypochondriacs whom he normally indulged. Mrs Barnaby, Mrs Comey Smith and little Tommy Keswick were all well qualified for this classification and knew what to do in such circumstances. On hearing the fracas from behind the consulting room door they would each make their excuses and hastily vacate the waiting room. Naturally, it was important not to lose face with fellow villagers who were present, lest you be thought a malingerer and not truly in need of the doctor's services. Thus these departures were accompanied with announcements such as: "I just remembered I promised my daughter I'd get her a wholemeal loaf. Better get to the bakers before they are sold out. I'll be back tomorrow." Or "Nearly forgot. I was going to catch the bus into town this morning. Think I'll come back tomorrow." Of course, these theatricals were wasted on most villagers who knew perfectly well who regularly wasted the doctor's time. Indeed, these three – and there could well have been others – were very much products of the coming of The National Health as it is known around here. Prior to this advance in health care those beset with some malady who went 'up the Doc's' would be charged anything between sixpence and five shillings for the consultation and medication, depending on how Gates viewed their financial state. Even though he was extremely generous with the poorer families in the neighbourhood, the fact that there was a charge acted as a deterrent to those who were not truly in need of his services. All this changed dramatically with the coming of The National Health when the likes of the three hypochondriacs could not only indulge their imagined illnesses for free but turn the doctor's waiting room into a meeting place for regular gossip and observation. For some, other people's ills are an absorbing interest, and what better place to become familiar with the ailments of others than a doctor's waiting room. I assume that Gates tolerated these individuals because numbers counted under health service administration, although when he was really busy these characters were soon in and out of his room, usually clutching a bottle of something or other; placebos one suspects.

In the old days Doctor Gates did his own dispensing – or appeared to – as bottles and boxes of the various medicines he passed out were ready on a side table in his consulting room. In the early days of The National Health a woman who wore a white overall coat was involved in this task on a part-time basis. Her presence marked a deterioration in service, in that whereas Doctor Gates would in most cases be able to bestow the appropriate medicine at the conclusion of his diagnosis, the patient now had to wait for 'her in the white coat' to make up the prescription, which meant more time in the waiting room until she had done this, or coming back to collect later in the day. Among the frequently dispensed 'mixtures' was a bottle containing a thick white substance for sufferers of tummy upsets, irreverently known by the villagers as Doctor Gates' Turd Binder, and one containing a pale brown liquid for constipation, acknowledged in similar fashion as Doctor Gates' Runs Maker. As a small boy I had experience of both and confirm their efficacy.

While the three notable hypochondriacs may have been preoccupied with their own health, they were no less interested in that of others. Both Mrs Comey Smith and Mrs Barnaby exhibited unabashed cheek when it came to the reasons for other people's visits to the surgery and had no hesitation in asking anyone they knew why they were there if the information wasn't forthcoming voluntarily. Mrs Barnaby's nosiness was well known and behind her back she was often referred to as Snouty. Mrs Comey Smith was likewise known as Snouty's Mate. Mrs Barnaby was a large ruddy faced woman who, judging by the way she sucked sweets while in the waiting room, had no worries about being over-weight. In contrast, Mrs Comey Smith was as thin as a rake; a pale, bespectacled woman who never seemed to be devoid of a head scarf. It is probably unfair to link little Tommy Keswick with them for he rarely got a word in edgeways, apart from when the women consulted him on some specific matter. Most of his contribution to the gossip session was taken up with nods and chuckles, or if he was lucky the odd "Thas right." Sometimes Tommy volunteered a "He didn't ..." or a "She look . . ." before being cut short by one of the women. Tommy had a habit of rocking to and fro on his seat, particularly when he was trying to enter the conversation but could not penetrate the verbal flow of the two busybodies. If Barnaby and Smith were already in the waiting room when he arrived they almost always acknowledged him with a "How's your problem, Tommy?" Tommy's response was invariably "Not so bad." I never did know what Tommy's 'problem' was that made him a frequent visitor 'up the Doc's' for many years.

The trio rarely missed a Saturday morning and were simply using the waiting room as a place to exchange gossip. Having exhausted the current topics and seen who else was visiting, they would sometimes depart without seeing the doctor. Discussing other peoples ills was all very well if quietly performed with due discretion, but Mrs Barnaby and Mrs Comey Smith not only carried on in brazen fashion but in voices loud enough for everyone else in the waiting room to hear. One Saturday morning they were in particularly strident mood.

"Mrs Riddlestone were in here Monday. Proper wheezy she were. Thas her lungs you know. Her old mother were just the same. Soon as that turn cold she'd be havin' trouble gettin' her breath. You remember her, don't you Tommy? Lived on the corner of Friar's Lane."

"Yes, she. . . ."

"They couldn't do nothin' for her. Anyway, the family got a cheap funeral 'cause they were related to Charlie Gaybarrow and he didn't charge for diggin' the grave."

"Girl Bull were in here yesterday – with her mum!" Knowing looks all round. "Can you wonder. She been seen with that eldest boy of Edie Mortlake's. Ain't that so, Tommy?"

But of course, Tommy could not get in an affirmation before being talked down.

At this juncture Bill Stokes, who ran the village taxi, entered the waiting room. He had probably deliberately delayed his attendance in order to avoid the nosy parkers. Unfortunately there had been a pretty full waiting room that morning and a half dozen or so were still waiting to see Gates. Stokes had only just sat down when Mrs Barnaby called out across the room: "How are you getting along with your piles, Bill?"

Plainly the man was embarrassed and only mumbled an incoherent reply. After all piles are very personal; not the sort of infliction one wants to have discussed by those unaffected.

"Thas something painful, I been told. You sittin' about all day in that old car of yours don't help, I should think. Do that make it worse?" Mrs. Comey Smith chipped in but the only response was a grunt. More sensitive individuals would have noticed the embarrassed flush on Bill Stokes' cheeks and changed the subject, but not these blinkered matrons.

"You've had 'em a couple of months now, ain't you ? I hope you arn't a bleedin' much?" Mrs Barnaby pressed.

The affronted man did utter a sharp "No", his embarrassment now turned to suppressed anger. At this moment the situation was relieved by a woman leaving the inner sanctum and Mrs Barnaby's turning attention to her welfare, while Mrs Comey Smith went in to see the doctor. Smith was not long in the consulting room and on her exit she informed her friend, who was next in the queue: "You'll have to come back if he want you to have some medicine, 'cause her in the white coat has only just turned up for work."

Bill Stokes had to wait a good three-quarters of an hour for his turn to see the doctor, and he was the last of the morning surgery. When he entered Gates asked him if Mrs Barnaby and Mrs Comey Smith were still in the waiting room and was told they were not. All had gone. Stokes saw that the reason for this question was that 'her in the white coat' had emerged from the little dispensing cubicle holding two small bottles, the contents of one being white and of the other brown. The significance of these was not lost on Bill Stokes who, like just about everyone else in the parish, had been a recipient of these well known mixtures for digestive problems. He saw his chance for revenge.

"They asked me to take 'em if they was ready."

"All right then. Put the bottles on the desk, my dear, and Mr Stokes will deliver them after our consultation" Gates instructed 'her in the white coat'.

The following Monday morning Doctor Gates found the first to enter at surgery time was Mrs Barnaby. Gates was in a particularly good mood, if a little surprised that one of his regulars should come back so soon.

"Its me diarrhoea, doctor. Thas got ten times worse not better. That stuff you sent me ain't done no good at all. That ain't like the stuff you usually give out, different colour."

She held out the half empty bottle. Gates took it, read the label, turned the bottle round, looked at it again and placed it on his desk. He then got up and went towards the dispensary: "Just wait awhile and I'll get you something better that will help." After less than a minute he returned with another bottle containing a white mixture. "Here you are, Mrs Barnaby. This should clear the trouble up."

The woman looked at the bottle: "This is like what you usually give for diarrhoea. Was the other lot a mistake?" Only Liz Barnaby would have the nerve to suggest the doctor had made a mistake, but Gates only smiled and replied: "We are trying out different medicines all the time. Sometimes they work, sometimes they don't."

Gates was not surprised when Mrs Comey Smith appeared before him later that morning. or when she presented a bottle with partly used white contents. Nor was he surprised when she complained that her constipation was much worse and that she hadn't been able to 'go' at all since taking the dose he had directed. The dispenser had arrived and was asked by Gates to produce another medicine to prescription; this time it was a light brown colour. Mrs Barnaby had waited for her friend and they left the surgery together speculating that 'her in the white coat' had put the labels on the wrong bottles.

"I bet Gates will give her an earful for mixing the labels up. If she'd knocked on my door instead of leavin' it on the step I'd have queried that medicine when I saw the colour. Thought that were somethin' new; thas why I took it."

Doctor Gates had no cause to admonish his dispenser. He had seen the labels on the bottles the women returned were held with a thick whitish glue, whereas the labels when applied were ready-gummed and only had to be moistened to make them adhere. He assumed that Stokes considered this a practical joke. As letting a patient deliver medicines for another might be questioned as bad practice he evidently decided to say nothing to Stokes.

All this happened at a time when a new method of treating piles had recently superseded the old. Apart from being relatively painless, the new method was quickly effective. Bill Stokes had been started on the new process but Gates decided the old method, which was not only painful but entailed prolonged treatment over several weeks, would be more suited to Stokes' particular condition.

The Days of Slap and Tickle

"Things have come to a pretty pass with this sectional harrowing – or whatever they call it – ain't they?"

Old Newson may have been hoping for a mardle as I passed his cottage but he was going to be unlucky this time. I kept walking as I pondered his greeting. There was no wish on my part to defend the latest agricultural practices, yet curiosity got the better of me:

"Is that some new cultivation technique or a new type of harrow?"

"Yer know damn well what I'm on about. The case in the old East Anglian Daily Times today, about the gal what got a thousand pounds just 'cause her boss tripped on the office carpet and accidentally grabbed her lallies to stop himself fallin'."

"Oh, you mean sexual harassment," I exclaimed, limiting my amusement to a smile and continuing on my way.

"I knew it were somethin' like that. Don't hold with these new fangled words. That were slap and tickle in my day and there's not much wrong with that."

"I think there was a bit more to this particular case. It's all to protect women," I preached.

"In my day gals could look after themselves. They'd soon give you a smack on the chops if they didn't like what you was doin'," old Newson called after me. Then as a parting thought he shouted: "Wouldn't have done for Rue Scrutts to be up to his tricks now, would it?"

"No," I called back, laughing.

Rue Scrutts having seen ninety is hardly a sexual threat to women even if he is still vocal on connected subjects. He has long been categorised as a dirty old man by those village women who have forsaken both femininity and sexuality for a neuter role. How far his coarse tongue was actually matched by comparative deeds in his younger days, I know not, although even then I fancy it was usually more talk than do. Yet old Newson's observation was certainly correct, for I can recall some of Rue's escapades with land girls that would most certainly have had him in court nowadays.

During 'the war' the Guv'nor employed several members of the Women's Land Army, the turnover being fairly rapid when many found that farm work was far from an idyllic livelihood. Most farm tasks entailed prolonged physical effort which many young women were simply not up to. The hard graft of the labour intensive agriculture of those days was truly man's work. The Guv'nor, appreciating the physical limitations of these girls, tried to give them the lighter jobs or restrict to the time spent on more strenuous activity.

The coming of these young women in green sweaters and light brown breeches to our farm was a novelty for Rue, Wully and the others. Hitherto about the only time members of the fair sex were seen on the farm in a working capacity was when a gang came to pick potatoes, occasions not enjoyed by the regular staff who found nothing fair about these spud Amazons. The WLA girls came from all walks of life, many from urban situations finding it difficult to adjust to the raw behaviour of the farmyard. The Guv'nor did his best to mellow the shock by not involving them in overseeing the mating of animals and telling the men to watch their language and conduct. But men being men and Rue being Rue the girls came in for a deal of badinage. Occasionally a bit of rough and tumble too, as I will tell.

The coming of the threshing tackle put a heavy demand on farm labour. A gang of eight was required in addition to the two contractor's men who came with the set to feed in the sheaves and monitor the machinery. On these occasions I was allowed to stay away from school to man the chaff box, such was the dearth of labour. My dislike of school is plain, for the chaff box was considered the worst of the threshing jobs. It only required the filling of sacks with chaff from the box and pulling them away, but the position was always beset with heavy dust that stung the eyes and blocked the nose. A coal miner was not as grimed as a chaff box minder after a day's toil. No great physical effort was required, but the Guv'nor thought the task too awful for a land girl to undertake.

In November 1942 the threshing tackle arrived to deal with four large wheat stacks, which meant a week off school at the chaff box for this then fourteen-year-old. The steam engine chugged, the drum hummed and the straw elevator clack-clacked away, distinctive sounds in the countryside when grain was still cut with a binder. I suffered at the chaff box, at first shut in by the drum on one side and the stack on the other. As the latter was gradually reduced in size so my environment and outlook improved and by the lunch break the sheaf pitchers had taken the stack down to a level about three feet from the ground. Those with pitch forks were Wully, Rue and a land girl called Penny. A tall, slim brunette, Penny had worked in a London office, yet despite her background and physique she exhibited a willingness to engage in this muscle-taxing task without complaint. Nevertheless, the Guv'nor thought fit to alternate Penny with another land girl, Rosie, a day pitching and a day in the dairy, to give each a break.

I had observed that unlike the stack-wise Wully and Rue, Penny did not have the leg bottoms of the fawn bib-and-brace overalls tied tight with string. The bottom of a corn rick was usually infested with mice and rats, particularly if the stack had stood through the winter. Boys armed with sticks would usually gather to slaughter the rodents as a form of sport as much as pest control. The terrified creatures had been known to seek cover up trouser legs on many occasions, hence the protective string. When Rue returned from his lunch I remarked on the fact that Penny hadn't tied the bottom of her trouser legs and was rebuked thus: "Don't you go a-tellin' on her that when she come back. Just you keep your young trap shut. We may have some sport along of her."

My interest primed, between changing chaff bags I kept a eye on the diminishing stack. As the final layer of sheaves were wrested from their positions and pitched up to the feeder on top of the threshing drum I spotted the first mouse scamper away into the pile of filled chaff bags. Then I saw what Rue intended: when Penny's back was turned he quickly bent down and picked up something. As she went to raise another sheaf, still with her back to Rue, he bent down again and put the mouse onto the sock under one leg of her trousers. Penny continued to pitch and I suspected the mouse had gone back into the stack. Then she suddenly dropped her fork and ran a hand down her thigh before turning to Wully with a look of horror: "There's something in my overalls!"

"Thas probably a mouse," said Wully, with a grin. The reaction was amazing. The girl let out a piercing scream and continued to scream in between crying: "Help me. I can't bear mice."

Of course, the gallant Rue came to the rescue, although I doubt he had expected Penny to be so allergic to mice: "Hold you hard, gal. I'll soon have that out of there. Where is it?"

Without waiting to be told where, Rue began to search the horror-struck girl on the outside.

"Ah, here's the little bugger. I'll have to put me hand inside your dungarees to get him," which he did. "There he goes. I'll get him. Never you mind dear, he won't hurt yer." From my vantage point it was obvious that Rue was taking the opportunity to conduct a thorough search for his hands were going everywhere. Finally, with a triumphant "I got 'im!" his hand was withdrawn and the mouse held up for the victim to see.

Some people have a thing about reptiles, others spiders. Penny's phobia was rats and mice, and such was her distress she fled from the stack, later to complain that if anyone had told her corn stacks were infested with mice and that they ran up trouser legs she would have refused to pitch. As for Rue, he went about chuckling to the other men: "I proper enjoyed myself, I did. You'd be surprised where that little owd mouse got to."

The following day Rosie joined Wully and Rue to pitch the next stack in line. The tackle had been moved up late the previous afternoon and I was again hemmed in between the chaff box and the stack. Before we started Rue sidled up to me and in lowered voice warned: "Don't you go sayin' anything to Rosie about what happened yesterday, boy. She ain't seen Penny so we might have some fun today too." As the girls were in different lodgings I was not surprised that Penny's predicament was unknown to Rosie. Nor was I surprised to see that Rosie did not have the bottom of her trouser legs tied round. Rosie was a different build to Penny. Chubby, you might say, and probably appearing more so due to her lack of height. While Penny's pitching pace had been about one sheaf to every three put up by the men; Rosie could nearly match them and did not appear to tire.

By the lunch break the stack was down to perhaps only two or three layers of sheaves and some mice had already started to run. Rosie didn't seem to mind them. I waited for Rue to make his move but all I got was a wink. Perhaps he had changed his mind or intended to wait until after the break. The latter proved to be the case, for the drum had not been humming for more than a couple of minutes before I saw Rue stoop and pick up a mouse and immediately transfer it to the bottom of Rosie's right trouser leg while she was turned away from him.

"Whoops! There's something going up my leg," she shouted to Rue.

"Hold hard, gal, I reckon thas a mouse. Where is it?" As yesterday, Rue had already started to run his hands up and down the victim without waiting for the invitation.

"I think it's here," giggled Rosie, indicating her waist. "Quick, get it out, its tickling."

No fear of mice with this girl, obviously. Thus encouraged Rue's hands were in hot pursuit under her shirt and heaven knows where. In contrast to Penny, Rosie was convulsed with laughter: "Oh, careful. You're tickling." And whereas Penny had been rooted to the spot, Rosie cavorted about, adding her own searching hands to Rue's, pulling out her shirt and shaking her dungarees. The mouse or Rue must have come to a very ticklish spot for with an extra loud shreik of laughter Rosie toppled over onto the sheaves, pulling Rue down with her.

It was at this point that the Guv'nor happened to arrive on the scene with a disapproving frown. "A mouse ran up her leg; she asked me to catch it," Rue exonerated himself. As Rosie made no complaint and only continued to giggle, the Guv'nor shrugged his shoulders and moved on. Naturally, when the stack was finished and Rosie was gone home, Rue smugly boasted of his enterprise in his usual crude terms adding: "I never did find that mouse. I dare say thas gone to earth. We'll know if she complain of constipation tomorrow."

It may not have been the morrow but a day or so later as I was walking through the farmyard on my return from school that Penny called to me from the cart lodge. Rosie was with her.

"You saw what happened when we were threshing the other day. Did Rue Scrutts deliberately put those mice up our trousers?" I must have flushed red as I procrastinated over an answer. "Come on, tell us the truth. We won't tell him you told us," Penny insisted. I have always been weak with women and this must have been an early example of my frailty, for I told all. The girls were not amused, not even Rosie, who uttered all sorts of nasty threats as to what she would like to do to certain parts of Rue's anatomy, indirectly expanding my schoolboy knowledge of such matters. I felt a traitor to the male cause for weeks afterwards, although I am certain Rue never knew I had split on him in view of what happened next.

For some reason which I forget, my return from school in the local town was later than usual the following day. No sooner had I entered the house than the Guv'nor approached me in stern mood and started a verbal chastisement for an assumed dangerous prank I had played on Rue. I pleaded innocent and finally convinced him that I was not the culprit. Rue was always the first to arrive for work in the morning and unlocked the workshop door. The key was kept on top of the wall inside the lodge. This day on reaching up to get it in the gloom what Rue got was a mouse trap round his fingers. Not the usual light type but the larger strong-spring version that would do for rats as well. As a result Rue had some very sore and bruised fingers. He and everyone else on the farm was convinced only the Guv'nor's wayward son would engage in such a dangerous prank. Fortunately I was able to remind the Guv'nor that he was in the workshop the previous night while I was doing my homework. Unless he thought I had climbed out of my bedroom window for a twenty feet drop to the ground it could not have been me. The trap with key was surely set in the morning before Rue came to work and he must have caught his fingers in it before I left the house for school. Thus was my innocence proved and much dark speculation initiated among the farm staff as to the villain.

Unhappily I remained the number one suspect as all believed the Guv'nor had been hoodwinked. Really hurtful, and much to my surprise, the prime advocates of this were Penny and Rosie. When an opportunity arose and they were on their own I attempted to obtain a confession, only to have them both harangue me with what a cowardly brat I was not to own up. They did not disguise their amusement very well while doing this and I was darn sure they were the guilty ones. The rotters; and to think I was the one who told them what Rue was up to. After this episode I was truly wary of the duplicity of women!

Wully's Win

Wealth is power, in its broadest sense. Being wealthy affords the individual an independence from the usual strictures that mark our passage through life in a developed society. Many deny any wish to be wealthy, but should this state come upon them few would not use it to advantage to meet their dreams. Indeed, for the majority, participation in the national lottery is the pleasure derived from imagining how to use the winning millions, even though the event is highly unlikely to occur. It is also an escape route from a routine job or restrictive life style through the thrill of a gamble.

Before the lottery, the fotball pools offered large rewards against a small investment, and this is still a preferred attraction for a majority of gamblers. For most of their working lives every male member of our farm staff indulged with a few shillings, and more recently pounds, in the hope of getting that winning line of draws.

In more than a half century I know only of one person in this district who won a relatively large sum on 'the pools', and that was our Wully. True, there may have been others who won and kept it secret, as I am sure Wully would have done had he not overlooked the 'no publicity' box on his coupon that particular week. He was certainly taken aback and overawed by the pools company representative who descended with cheque and cameraman a day or two after Wully had made his claim. The secret was out and everyone in the village knew that Mr William Snow of No. 2 Thistledown Cottages had won the sum of three thousand, one hundred and six pounds, fifteen shillings and eightpence for his winning line. In the final years of the twentieth century this would hardly raise an eyebrow, but in the late nineteen-fifties, before inflation ran wild, it was a not inconsiderable amount, sufficient to buy a small house and a car and still leave a goodly lump over.

Among the first to congratulate Wully and offer advice was the Guv'nor. The stalwart farm labourer and one time cowman had by that date worked for him for a good twenty years, the Guv'nor's concern being that having previously only known an agricultural wage Wully might fall prey to some smooth talking trickster eager to relieve him of his new found wealth. Wully was known to be headstrong, cocky and on occasions tetchy. The grumpiness came with any prolonged perambulation. He would pitch sheaves or hay energetically all day and be of happy disposition, but plodding behind a horse drawn implement or similar activity involving several hours of walking was not conducive to his good humour, probably because he suffered from fallen arches. He usually kept his own counsel and rarely sought advice, so the Guv'nor thought him vulnerable in this new-found situation. He could not have been more wrong.

"I don't want to interfere Wully, but if you need any advice on your money I'll be happy to help," the Guv'nor proffered. "There are a lot of sharks around and I wouldn't want to see you taken for a ride."

"There's no need to worry on my score, Guv'nor. No one is gonna twist me."

"You can afford to buy yourself a house now for your old age. Fenney might be willing to sell you the one where you live for a few hundred." Even though advice had not been requested the Guv'nor was determined to give some.

"What do I want to own a house for? There's only me and the missus and we've no relations to leave it to when we go. I'm quite content to pay Fenney his five shillings a week rent. There's a lot of trouble that goes with houses and I don't want the bother of it," Wully responded.

"If the house was yours you would be able to improve it – have a modern kitchen fitted to help your wife."

"Blast, she's always sayin' she ain't got enough to do now so she wouldn't want things any different. 'Sides we don't hold with all these new gadgets: they're always goin' wrong. Just more trouble."

In view of this emphatic reply the Guv'nor took a different line: "Why not buy yourself a little car. You can drive a tractor so you'd soon get the hang of a car. Take your wife out and go shopping or visiting."

"We can do all the shoppin' we want around here and there ain't nobody we want to visit, so why do I want a car. Just expense and trouble and I wouldn't pass me test for a licence at my age. 'Sides my old feet wouldn't be too good on the pedals and I'd be for ever knockin' people arse over head."

"Then why don't you take your wife away on holiday somewhere?" The Guv'nor didn't get an opportunity to enlarge on this suggestion as Wully, by now slightly irritated cut in:

"Holiday? What do we want with a holiday? Blast we don't know what to do at a weekend now, so the last thing we'd want is waste money goin' somewhere else to do nothin'."

The Guv'nor could not quite follow the logic of this but decided it was a hopeless cause and offered one final piece of advice: "Well, at least you can put the money in a building society and that will earn interest for you and will be there when you decide what you want."

"Don't want nothin' to do with buildin' societies or the likes. That's in my Post Office Savings account and there that stays." Wully's annoyance now plain to see, the Guv'nor gave up on his good intentions and talked farming tasks.

While Wully obviously didn't want any advice on his wealth, if he was not going to use it to better his life style one could not help wondering why so many years were spent trying to win the pools. He continued to work on the farm until retiring six years later and during this period there was never the slightest sign of his tapping capital. Sadly, not long after, his wife had a stroke and died. Everyone expected Wully to use the money to better his lot now he was on his own, yet he was quite content to carry on just as before. About a couple of years on, word went round that Wully had a housekeeper;

the old miser had come to his senses at last. But it was not to endure, for within a fortnight the village gossip line reported Wully's housekeeper had left. One morning, seeing Wully at work in his garden I deliberately went in to pass the time of day – well, to be honest my curiosity had the better of me.

After the usual chit-chat about the weather and so on, I casually commented: "Hear you had a housekeeper for a while."

Indignation marked the "Soon got rid of her!" response.

I deliberately chose my words to provoke: "Didn't she do her work properly or didn't you pay her enough?"

"Pay her! I ain't payin' people to do what I can do myself! She got her pension just as I got mine and I was givin' her a free roof over her head. That were the arrangement when she come. Nibby Tegget said he got a widowed sister-in-law that were lookin' for accommodation in exchange for doin' the housework and cookin'. So I takes her on but that were a big mistake."

"Oh, why?" I admit to being intrigued.

"Second night she were there I'd just got into my bed when she come in and tries to get in with me! Says she thought as it were a cold night I might need warmin' up. I says forty year ago, gal, I would have dragged you in, but I'm warm enough , thank yer. Pulls the blankets around me tight and that put a stop to her little game. Dang me, next night when I come up stairs if she ain't already in my bed. Ha, I don't get caught out that easy. I goes and gets into her bed and bolts the door! I soon realised what her game was."

"What was that?" My interest was now blatantly nosey.

"I know about these women that try and get you between the sheets and the next thing is you got to marry them. That's what she got in mind. She were tryin' to get her hands on my nest egg but I see what she's up to." There was a distinct note of triumph in Wully's final sentance.

"Don't really think you had to worry about having to marry her at your ages. She may just have been trying to be friendly. Probably doesn't even know about your winnings."

"She knew all right. They all know round here and is for ever stickin' their noses in askin' how I'm goin' to spend it. They'd all like to get their hands on a bit of that but they're goin' to be unlucky 'cause that stay right where it is!"

The temptation to ask where was resisted, as well it should have been. At least I was now convinced that like many people who had come into money, it was not so much a case of frugality with Wully, rather the enormous pleasure of having a tidy sum tucked away. Even so, I could not resist a piece of unsolicited advice, hackneyed as it was: "You might just as well spend it Wully. Enjoy yourself while you can. You can't take it with you."

"I'm enjoying myself, don't you worry. You're like your father; he were always givin' me advice on what to do with my winnings. I don't mean no offence: when I want advice I'll ask for it."

Wully passed away when in his late 'seventies. As he had said, years before, there were no living relatives on either his or his wife's side. The Inland Revenue were to be the beneficiaries of his wealth or so it seemed until a detective inspector arrived at my door. As Wully had worked for both my father and myself he wondered if I could throw any light on what happened to the three thousand pounds that were won but never spent. Apparently a few weeks before he died Wully had personally withdrawn all his savings down to the last penny in cash. His cottage had been turned upside down and there was no sign of any notes or record of disposal. Could it have been stolen or hidden? Neither. Wully was too wily for that. The money must have gone somewhere. Charities perhaps? Who knows. I doubt if anyone ever did but Wully. And what business was it of ours? After all, they were his winnings.

Horse Sense

Dealers have always been part of the agricultural scene, if less diverse in specialities than in the first half of this century when there were four times as many farmers in Britain as in its closing years. In livestock sector parlance a dealer is one who both buys and sells to his own advantage outside the established market sources. In East Anglia with its diminishing number of livestock farms, dealers in cattle and sheep are now few and far between, while the heavy horse dealer is no more. The carthorse, for long the motive power on all farms, disappeared rapidly in the decade following the Second World War, supplanted by the modern tractor with its pulling ability acknowledging its predecessor by being calculated in horse power. The handsome Suffolks, Percherons and Shires became a rarity in the fields, their presence now viewed with nostalgia by many of those who are old enough to have worked with them, particularly whenever a tractor breaks down. While I willingly acknowledge the beauty of these fine animals, my own youthful memories of carthorses on this farm are that they gave the Guv'nor more worries than any early tractor. A bold statement, for anyone who has had the task of starting a standard Fordson on a damp winter's morning knows that early tractors taxed one's patience and stamina to the limit.

The chief problem with our horses was that they were brought in from elsewhere and never bred or trasined on our farm. In spite of the dealer's assurance that a horse was in good health and had no nasty habits, such frequently manifested themselves. Complaining to the dealer concerned invariably brought a hurt plea of "You're not thinking I would twist you? I want to do business with you again and I wouldn't sell you a dud. That horse was sold in good faith. Never had any problems before that I know of." The Guv'nor wasn't usually gullible but he did tend to give people the benefit of the doubt a little too often, and the more devious knew this and were not slow in taking full advantage.

George Woodbridge was the dealer who ingratiated himself with the Guv'nor to the extent that they were on first name terms and George was 'a good sort' who could be relied upon. He even took one horse back that we found had a limp. He really had no option as the animal was in the process of being unloaded from the horsebox on delivery when this was first noticed. Those farm men who had to work with horses supplied by George Woodbridge generally held a different view, even if their caustic comments did little to deflect the Guv'nor from his trust in this dealer's judgement. Not even the case of Matilda.

Matilda was a fine three-year-old Suffolk mare, about eighteen hands and supposedly from a good home, the previous owner having retired from farming, so Woodbridge said. Not many weeks after it arrived both Rue and Wully reported the horse occasionally having wheezing bouts. Then one day Matilda was pulling a tumbrel up a slight incline when the mare collapsed in the shafts, reducing the land girl who was leading it to tears. The vet was called and pronounced the horse unfit for further work, due to broken wind.

George Woodbridge was most concerned when the Guv'nor telephoned him. The horse had been sold in good faith and the previous owner had never had any trouble; the problem must have developed in the ten months it had worked on our farm. The Guv'nor could 'phone the former owner if he wished: Woodbridge offered the telephone number. Of course, Woodbridge's word was good enough for the Guv'nor, particularly when the dealer said he had just the horse to replace Matilda, a real strong gelding, and as he was concerned about the trouble the Guv'nor had experienced the replacement would be put in at half price.

Didn't want to lose a good customer, so he said. As for Matilda, the Guv'nor being soft hearted kept it until the following summer for use on the hay rake and other light jobs. The wheezing got worse and twice the mare collapsed, once nearly on top of Wully who was particularly vocal about the incident much to our amusement. Eventually, the Guv'nor did what he should have done in the first place, sent the ailing horse off to the knackers. Sad, but such situations are inevitable with animals.

As for the replacement gelding, there was nothing amiss with its working ability. What was very much amiss for those of us who had to work with the brute was its proclivity for taking a bite out of anything or anyone. After the animal sank its teeth into a land girl the Guv'nor, fearful that one day someone might be seriously harmed, sent it back to Woodbridge in one of those complicated deals where we were supposed to be getting a bargain replacement. This one was a large white gelding, a placid creature, a bit long in the tooth, if a willing worker. Ideal for the land girls to handle, even if tumbrel journeys often took much longer to complete. The reason was eventually brought to Guv'nor's attention by an exceedingly frank land girl out of the East End who asked: "What's wrong with that bloody 'oss, Guv'nor? It keeps stopping to piss and it don't 'alf take its time." The answer was asked of McTegget the vet who said the problem was much like that which he suffered himself, particularly after imbibing in the local hostelries, and like him we would have to live with it. The stop-go white horse was retained and happily peed its way through life much to the exasperation of those who had to work with it, for no amount of verbal commands or smacking with a stick would budge it until the last drop was discharged.

Another of the horses bought from George Woodbridge was perfectly sound in body and limb, worked well, but had been trained to obey religious commands having come – according to George Woodbridge – from a convent farm. We were told that to make it move the required call was Alleluia, and to stop, Amen; which proved to be the case. Unfortunately, we were not told it had an aversion to blasphemy, as Wully discovered. Sitting on a tumbrel load of mangolds being taken to the cattle, he kept getting his Alleluias and Amens mixed up. Exasperated he cursed "Bloody hell, Alleluia" whereupon the horse took off as fast as it could go, the first rut crossed jerking loose the trip handle of the tumbrel and unloading mangolds and Wully into the mud. The horse didn't stop until it reached the farmyard.

Then there was the young mare the Guv'nor intended to breed. For two years the stallion came, only to be greeted with flying feet every time it approached the mare. As was usual on such occasions a farm gate was held as protection for the stallion until it was ascertained if the mare was receptive. Despite constant monitoring by those on the farm who knew about such matters they were never able to get "the right time" and the enterprise was finally abandoned. Not only did the Guv'nor get fed up with paying attendance money every time the stallion was brought by horsebox, but the man who came with the stallion was becoming increasingly concerned about the kicking he had to avoid. As this mare showed a definite interest in other mares it was known by a rather crude and uncomplimentary term by Rue and Wully, but not in the Guv'nor's hearing.

In the spring of 1946 George Woodbridge managed to persuade the Guv'nor to buy another Suffolk mare. The Guv'nor went to look at the beast and returned to inform us that it had no vices and was the best he'd seen for years. I think from the smell of his breath Woodbridge had clinched the deal with the help of the whisky bottle. Like me, the farm staff were sceptical, reserving their judgements, for we had not had a single horse from Woodbridge that was without some peculiarity. When the Suffolk was let out of the horsebox it appeared an attractive animal as it made straight for the water butt. I looked at Wully and Wully looked at me; we were obviously thinking the same thing. When the horse had finished drinking it turned and walked up the yard by itself and straight into the second stable.

"I don't believe it" was the Guv'nor's amazed exclamation.

"You better," said Wully, "thas Matilda; the one that had broken wind and was sent to the knackers."

The Guv'nor went all quiet, a sign he was raging inside. He could have stopped the haulier who was just driving out of the yard to make him take the horse back, but he didn't.

Of course, George Woodbridge was beside himself with apologies as he had 'sold the horse in good faith', which really meant he hadn't bothered to ask the farmer who sold it to him too many questions if he thought he had a bargain price. The real rogues were the knackers men who decided they could make more by selling Matilda to a farmer or dealer than for slaughter. No doubt over the two years absence from our farm it had passed through several hands as each had discovered the broken wind and craftily sold it on without mention of this malady. Matilda was fortunate because George Woodbridge having forgone payment as a penance, the Guv'nor didn't have the animal put down as he said he was going to do. Appearing less troubled than when we had her the first time, he kept the mare for light jobs. Actually, Matilda was little used and I fancy the Guv'nor developed a soft spot for her because she most certainly never paid her way and was pensioned off until expiring in a meadow on an autumn day in 1951. By that time the Guv'nor was into buying second-hand tractors. But that is another story.

Playing With Words

"He's struck again !"

Although taken unawares, I should have known that such a dramatic salutation from old Newson would be unlikely to be worthy of the facts. The mid-day sun burned down on the harvest field and with a respite from my task as grain haulier from combine to store, a lunch break had been taken in the shade of the rear tractor wheel. No doubt my movements were carefully monitored by the sage from his cottage garden ready so he could pounce as soon as it was opportune. Harry Newson does not easily pass up a chance for a mardle.

"Who's struck?" I spluttered, having been in the process of sinking my teeth into a cucumber sandwich. My question received no direct answer.

"You know Mrs Aidswell what live at the Grange have a TO LET notice outside the lodge cottage?"

"Yes, I have seen it," I gulped, swilling the remains of my first bite of sandwich down with tea from a flask.

"Well, he's put an I between the TO and the LET !" was old Newson's emphatic announcement.

"That's a schoolboy prank; as old as the hills."

"Thas where you're wrong," triumphed my informant, "He's painted it on just like the other letters and in the same shade of red. You wouldn't know that it weren't a toilet sign."

"Maybe, but everyone knows a lodge cottage isn't a . . ." Old Newson obviously anticipated my response and cut me short with:

"Arr! Thas where you is forgettin' them foreigners we're always seein' around here now that come from that Common Market. If one of them is wantin' to go and sees that sign, they'll soon be out of their car and be. . . ." It was my turn to interject, knowing old Newson's tendency to give unnecessarily graphic details on matters of relief and I did not want to be put off my hazelnut yogurt.

"Has anyone told Mrs Aidswell?" My question was ignored, as I feared it would be, for the subject was not abandoned.

"You've forgot what happened to Walter Clark, Honker Clark's brother what live up Dell Lane. Him that have a board outside his front gate advertisin' what he's got for sale from his garden. His owd carrots is somethin' good and he don't charge a lot. Anyways, don't you remember when he'd got bunches of lavender for sale but as he didn't know how to spell lavender he just chalked LAV on the bottom of his board? Next thing he knew when he come out of his back door there's a grut owd German gal boppin' down behind his currant bushes and a grinnin' at him. You can't take no chances with them from the eck. Dirty lot. They'll go anywhere."

It seemed prudent to agree although I took a little while to realise that "the eck" was my mentor's verbal rendering of the E.E.C. By this time old Newson had rested his rear end on the front tractor tyre, a convenient perch used before for conducting one of his lectures on village matters past and present. At least on this occasion I knew that once the combine grain tank was full and had to be emptied I would have good reason to terminate the session and be on my way.

"Did you hear what he did last Saturday week? You know there's a board outside the Wheelright's Arms that say what bar meals is on that day. He altered the I to an E in SHEPHERD'S PIE. The new landlord at the Wheelrights didn't know anything about it and kept wondering why them in the bar kept a laughin' and sayin' as how he was at last bein' honest about his beer. Proper vexed he was when he found out."

The 'he' referred to was the perpetrator of a spate of alien word changing on signs in the district; pranks which had flourished for a year or so, the cuprit or culprits undetected. Speculation as to who was responsible was a popular topic of conversation, particularly in local pubs.

"How do you know its a 'he'. It may be a 'she' and there is probably more than one person up to this sort of thing."

Such a suggestion found little favour with this arch male chauvinist: "No, that ain't what a woman would get up to. Women don't have that sort of clever learnin'. And thas got to be the same fellow 'cause the changes is always so neat. Ain't everyone who can paint careful like he do. Yes, thas got to be the same fellow and I've a good mind as to who he be; but I'm not a-sayin'!"

This was just old Newson's bluff so that he could spend the next few minutes in evasive dialogue bolstering his ego. I've known Harry Newson long enough to know that if he had the slightest suspicion as to the culprit he would have been very willing to air his views. As I didn't take the bait and continued to spoon yogurt out of its little plastic pot into my mouth the village oracle launched into a survey of all the phantom word fiddler's activities that had been brought to his notice: "Reckon that were Billy Hastings' PICK YOUR OWN notice where he first struck. 'Course, Billy take his time over everything and that were a couple of weeks before he got around to painting out the NOSE that had been added. Next thing that were got at were them little SOFT VERGE notices the owd council workmen stuck in when they did up the main road. You know what Rue Scrutts called out to me when he was a biking past to the pub: 'Don't know of any virgins round here let alone any soft oncs'. Thought that were a real laugh, did Rue, and you'd think he were long past takin' an interest in anything like that. Then there were all that fuss about what was put over the football club's place; they say that were done the same night as the F were added to the sign over the Art Centre door. Mind you, knowing owd Ludington-Witt what run it, that weren't far off the mark." A pause for a laugh and a dab at his mouth with the familiar spotted handkerchief and the catalogue continued. "That were a bit bad what

he did to the PLEASE SHUT on the door to the school lavatory. Head mistress called the bobby about that but he don't know who is doin' it no more than I do."
"Thought you said you knew who it was?" I couldn't resist getting that in quickly but, unpertered, old Newson snapped back: "No I din't. I

said I thought I knew and thas quite different!" And to make sure he was not taken to task further on this point the survey was quickly continued: "Weren't very nice what he did to HOPE JENNINGS hairdressers sign. They say he must have had a ladder to get up there and add LESS. Poor woman were something upset when she saw it. What tickled me more than any was what he did to the NO ENTRY notice what them toffee nosed lot who live where the Gilfords did have put up at the end of one of their drives. He got that right 'cause they certainly aren't gentry even if they think they be."

The tank-full light on the combine was flashing. "Must go," I said. "Can't hold Tim up." Old Newson removed his posterior from the tractor wheel, turned, grubbed his stick into the stubble and leant forward on it, watching as I climbed into the cab, and then called out: "You want to watch out he don't do some work on the name of your tractor. He could proper spice that up!"

I laughed and brought the tractor engine to life.

The phantom sign mutilator's activities have long since ceased. He or she probably tired of the activities or grew up - or both. Occasionally I still puzzle over what could be made of MASSEY FERGUSON without coming to a satisfactory conclusion. And somehow I don't think I'd get a straight answer from old Newson even if I were rash enough to ask him.

The Friday Fox

The fox made its unhurried way along the edge of the field, dodging between the withered patches of nettles. Close under the hedge it was often lost from view behind a bulge of brambles or a tumble of hawthorn hung with red hips. Down the hill he ambled, the pace increasing, until the early morning mist in the valley hid its progress. Little else moved as the sun highlighted the reds and yellows of the horse chestnut leaves and cast dark shadows where it was yet to reach.

Old Briar Smith knew that in a minute or two the fox would reappear beyond the stream, heading up the meadow beneath the dead elms in the ill-kept fence. He had spent a lifetime around these fields, woods and hedgerows and knew the ways of wild things better than some folk know their families. Indeed, he never had much time for his own family or they for him, an attitude which largely stemmed from his frequent absence from home when the boys were young and about. Three had long lived elsewhere in the country, and he had not set eyes on them for more than thirty years. They did not even come to their mother's funeral, such was the family disunity. Old Briar now lived with the fourth son, a Tesco minion, who moved into the family home ostensibly to 'look after father' but, as is often the case, father continued to look after himself.

For much of his working life old Briar had earned a living by finding and taking briar stock to a man who supplied rose nurseries. Most of the finding was done at first light when few others in the parish were awake, let alone abroad. Having always risen with the sun, he continued with the habit in retirement. When the sky began to lighten in the east Briar would be softly out of the kitchen door and out along the footpaths and lanes, just as he had done since George V was king. The son and his wife, while contemptuous of this activity, were pleased to have the old man out of the house for most of the day. And only the very worst weather would keep him in.

As Briar expected, it was not long before he spotted the brown-red of the fox pass by gaps in the far elm-lined meadow fence. Not quite as he expected, for the animal had chosen to go up the far side where it was less exposed in the brightening day. Old Briar had watched many a fox in his time, but what intrigued him about this one was what it carried in its mouth. When first seen from where he stood, the animal held something that was neither bird nor rabbit as it passed along the other side of the field. He was also surprised to see a fox carrying at this time of year, for there were no cubs to feed.

Briar moved away from the gnarled oak trunk which had hidden him into the field to obtain a better view; the fox was too far away now to be concerned about his presence. Briar knew where it was headed: the conifer wood at the top of the rise which concealed an earth. To get there from its present position the fox had to cross an open field of emerging wheat. The wily animal halted and remained motionless for a few seconds to check if it were safe before taking off across the fresh green of the seedlings. Although exposed, the fox did not increase its pace before finally disappearing from view into the wood.

The hedgerow veteran might not have given the occasion further thought had it not been for a near recurrence exactly a week later. This time while Briar was sat upon the old shooting stick he usually carried and positioned a little further down the same unruly hedge, a fox appeared. Once more it carried something in its mouth and followed more or less the same route down into the valley and up to the conifer wood. Briar brooded on the matter and for several successive mornings set himself up in the same location in the hope the fox might pass again. The weather then turned sour, and as the subject of his curiosity did not appear interest waned again.

The TV forecast was for fine days at the end of the week, although old Briar didn't need a pretty girl chattering away about lows and highs on that shimmering box to tell him what he knew from signs in the sky. He decided to amble down the lane and see if by chance the fox passed by. A Tesco plastic bag was taken along and he kept his promise to Harry Newson to pluck the blue sloes from a blackthorn so the sage could brew up one of his lethal concoctions. After the recent rain the mists rose heavy under an unusually warm late October sun. The valley was yet to be invaded by the sounds of man's noisy machines, and only the occasional yaffling of a green woodpecker winging between the trees broke the silence.

Then, there it was! The same dog-fox trotting down the far side of the field with that something in its mouth which old Briar could still not identify. Once more the creature made its way up to the far wood with its catch. Briar was annoyed: he had always prided himself that there was nothing he didn't know about the wild things hereabouts. Later, as he made off home with the bag of sloes, he suddenly realised that the day was a Friday, and the other two occasions he had seen the fox were also Fridays. Now his interest was really sparked.

During his quiet dawn wanderings over the next few days old Briar was given to puzzling out from whence the fox had come and planning where he should secrete himself to discover this. By the time the next Friday came round he had convinced himself that one of the urban-minded newcomers to the village was putting out food for the fox. A yuppie wife had done this a few years ago, until her cat was killed and eaten as hors d'oeuvres. It was whatever the fox carted home in its mouth that really tantalised, and why always around dawn?

Friday came wet and windy. The previous evening the daughter-in-law had told Briar 'not to be an old fool' and go out early if it was raining. "You'll catch your death of cold and we shall have to nurse you." The warning was lost on father-in-law. Fortunately dawn came windy rather than wet, which was to Briar's advantage as he could set himself up down-wind so the fox would not scent him. The problem was lack of cover, and which of the large fields that lay up towards the new housing estate the fox would come round. Briar mentally cursed the farmer who some years ago made three small fields into one of eighteen acres. Wherever he positioned himself the far hedgerow was too distant for a good look at the fox if it came. Having finally made up his mind and parked himself in a ditch, Briar settled in to wait.

The sky was overcast and the day long in taking hold. Now and then a strong gust from the south-west scattered the redundant leaves from a nearby sycamore. To keep warm Briar had donned a woollen scarf, gloves, and the army greatcoat he'd had ever since he was in the Home Guard. He had not been settled in the ditch more than five minutes scanning the far side of the stubble field when to his great surprise the fox passed just a few feet in front of him. The animal was even more surprised on coming upon a human at such close quarters and raced away down the field. All this happened so quickly that Briar only managed a fleeting glance at what was in the fox's mouth. He was not much the wiser, only that it appeared smooth and shiny and the fox appeared to be chewing or rolling whatever it was over in its mouth as it went.

It had been easy enough to slide down into the ditch; not so easy to get out. Age told, and two or three attempts were made before Briar successfully scrambled out. Standing for a few moments to regain his breath he noticed that not a light was to be seen in the houses on the estate. Turning, he saw that the only lights visible were further west at the Old Parsonage House, where Mrs McGregor had lived for many years and which was now a private hotel and restaurant. It now made more sense in Briar's mind that the fox had come from the direction of this latter establishment. However, his immediate concern was if the fox was sufficiently scared by their meeting to be wary of another return.

During the following days Briar's deductions following a mental review were worthy of a trained detective. Here was a wild and cunning animal engaged in carrying home some spoils at a similar time every Friday morning. An intelligence that took it to wherever it went at a precise time once a week was out of the question, so the fox must be attracted to linger, knowing that sooner or later that which it fancies will be available. The refuse collectors came to the village on a Thursday so it couldn't be something regularly put out for them. The most likely source was the hotel. Not only was it more or less in the direction he now thought the fox came from, but they might have foodstuff to dispose of on a Friday for some reason. Perhaps it wasn't food, for why should the fox carry it so far away? Briar did toy with the idea of hiding up in the hotel grounds until he remembered the owner had a large Labrador. But surely this would see the fox off too? Finally, he decided to seek out a member of the hotel staff and ask a few questions.

Briar was not one to confide in others, and while he did think of seeking Harry Newson's opinion when he took him the sloes, a wiser decision was made to say nothing. If word got out someone would soon be lying in wait for the fox with a gun. Briar had no love of foxes; he hadn't forgotten that one had slaughtered every hen in his chicken shed many years ago. Yet for the time being he was quite anxious to preserve this one's welfare. So when he asked the landlord at the Lamb if any of the folk who work at 'that place where posh people stay' ever came in for a drink, no mention of the reason for his interest was made. The answer was negative, as it was when he tried the Wheelright's Arms. It was an instance of third time lucky, for at the Anchor the landlady said the chef from the Old Parsonage Hotel occasionally came in for a drink on his day off, a Thursday. Briar now only went to a pub, usually the Lamb, at mid-day Sunday before dinner. However, such was his fascination with the Friday fox that for a bottle of sloe gin, obtained from Harry Newson, he persuaded the landlady to telephone his daughter-in-law when the chef next appeared in the pub and to ask her to tell Briar that his wallet had been found in the bar.

Good fortune again looked on Briar and his investigation, for the very next Thursday evening the 'phone call came. Ignoring the caustic comments of son and daughter-in-law about losing his wallet and warnings that a man of his age going out on a dark night was likely get run down by a car, Briar set off for the Anchor. The landlady pointed out a rotund, ginger-headed man in his forties sipping a scotch in the corner and talking with young Bramble Blake and another fellow Briar didn't know.

Briar was always one for coming straight to the point: "They tell me you're the cook at the Old Parsonage place. Do you put anything out of a Friday morning?"

The chef was a little bemused and got the wrong impression: "We do, but we're not allowed to give it away because that might not be fit for human consumption."

"I'm not after anything. I just wondered if you put anything out for a dog or cat?" old Briar pressed.

"As it happens I do. But what's all this about?" The chef was put on his guard, suspecting some complaint.

"Oh, nothin' much. Just that I thought I see a fox come out of your back hedge with something last Friday a little after seven in the morning."

The relief showed on the chef's face, and after taking a good gulp from his glass he revealed the answer to the foxy mystery: "It must have been after the sausages. The new supply is delivered about eight every Friday morning, so the first thing I do before getting breakfasts is to clear the 'fridge of any left over from the last lot – so they don't get mixed. I put them outside in the dog bowl. By the time that stupid retriever wakes up and gets off the boss's bed the packs are about thawed out. Thought that got through them quickly. Sometimes there's two or three packs put out if we haven't had many people in during the week. The fox must have found them a bit cold. We don't want him round there. In future I won't put the sausages out until the boss's dog is about. Thanks for telling us."

Briar did not enlarge on his statement, and after a half pint trudged home. He felt a little sad that by solving the mystery he had put an end to the fox's pleasure, and his own in seeing it pass so regularly. This proved to be the case, for although he kept watch on the three following Fridays there was no sign of the itinerant. A fox with an insatiable appetite for sausages that ran three-quarters of a mile to its earth, thawing out the pack by turning it over in its mouth as it went, might have been fact, but nobody was going to believe him. Briar was right, no one did.

The Sexist's Shoot

I am not a shooting man: that is, I get no pleasure out of potting the birds or the bunnies. Do not misunderstand me; neither am I one of those holier-than-thou types who proclaim that a human should not derive pleasure from skill with a gun in obtaining meat. It's not a case of objecting to the shooting sport; just the call of other interests. As a life-long countryman I must confess to having only once attended an organised shoot and that in recent times. It was certainly memorable.

Billy Hastings' son-in-law, Bob, arrived at my door with the request that I act as a beater for a shoot on the estate where he is manager. There were no longer enough employees on the estate to do the job and he had been unable to find many volunteers. He came to me because Group Captain Sir Edmund Huffie, who owns the Woodborne estate, was a great friend of my late uncle, another air force officer in the trouble with Hitler. Bob's niece, who lives in our village, would give me a lift there and back as she was helping with the refreshments. Although I protested my inexperience, a day in the beautiful countryside at Woodborne did appeal. Eventually persuaded, arrangements were made for his niece to collect me in her Volvo at eight the following Tuesday.

Happily the forecast was good and the day dawned bright, for the thought of flapping around in the rain was not encouraging. My transport arrived on time and a pleasant journey was enjoyed to Woodborne Hall, a grey Georgian mansion standing among the autumn golds of the park oaks. A pack of Land Rovers and other 'four by fours' were set before the house and numerous shooting types milled around on the gravel apron. Bob, having seen his niece's car arrive, was there to introduce me to the Group Captain, a form of address I had been told he preferred to his baronetcy as the former was earned and the latter inherited. We approached a wiry, balding, moustached and ruddy faced gentleman, exceedingly upright for his near eighty years. He was clad in a worn and faded battle-dress jacket, equally worn baggy trousers, the legs gathered into gaitered boots, all an indication that comfort was more important than show. To a cartridge belt around his waist were attached the leads of two large golden retrievers, the animals sitting patiently while their master conversed with those around him.

"Jolly good of you to come along, old bean," was the greeting that followed an introduction by Bob. My hesitation over the form of address as we shook hands brought a quick "Call me Groupy. Everyone does. What I prefer. Used to be Groupy the Groper but I'm too old for that now!" He twitched an end of his handle-bar moustache as he chuckled. "Expect Bob's told you we can't get the beaters. Three we usually have are laid up with some sort of wog flu, so he tells me."

I advised him that I had never done any beating.

"You a farmer and not interested in the birds? Extraordinary. Never mind old bean, I'm going to put you in Harry Jones' squad. Ex-RSM, capital chap. He'll put you wise. SIT GERT!" The thunderous roar was directed at one of the retrievers which had risen and strained on its lead. "Knew your uncle," Groupy continued, "Great pal of mine. One of the old school. Knew how to enjoy himself." I thought I detected a touch of nostalgia as he again rolled an end of his moustache with finger and thumb. Then, looking around he commented: "Mixed crowd here today; a few farmers and country friends but most of the guns are townies, they have the money nowadays, I'm afraid. Lot of chaps from the city. Rotten shots. Never get many birds. That's up to them. Sorry about the couple of gels. Don't hold with women handling guns but my stockbroker wanted them to come, says they've shot elsewhere and I gather they are in some financial concern and have done him a good turn."

I looked around and saw two very attractive and smartly dressed young women in the midst of a number of male admirers. Not the Barbour jacket and green wellies uniform sported by most urban ladies who venture into the sticks, but smart tailored outfits which even to my inexperienced eye must have cost a small fortune.

"A man's sport, shootin'. No place for gels," was Groupy's further emphatic comment. Then, brightening, he confided, "I'd only make one exception and that was old Bunty Forbes-Marshall. You may have heard your uncle talk of her? Lady in her own right but never used her title. Fantastic woman. Handle a twelve-bore as well as any man. I've known old Bunty knock down ten brace on a day's shoot and have the breeches of five fellows in the evening. She'd knock 'em down in the field or in the bedroom. Good with a rod too. Up on the Spey after salmon, was seducing her gillie when a storm rolled up. Creatin' so much energy, they attracted a bolt of lightening. Appropriate she should go out with a bang as she'd been banging away all her life! Ah yes, never be another Bunty! Well, must get on."

The anachronistic gentleman moved away to talk to others while I was taken to Harry Jones, who was to be the head beater. Now and then a severe SIT GERT or SIT DAISY rang out, the two retrievers evidently being named for two music hall comediennes of the 'forties. Presently we were all called to order and addressed by Groupy from the steps of the hall. It quickly became evident that the shoot was to be run on military lines. In what he referred to as his briefing, Groupy outlined the plan of action. The fourteen guns were given details of procedure and times for each of the eight drives planned that day, four before lunch and four after. Command signals from Groupy's police whistle were two short blasts to commence and one long blast to cease shooting. It did not go unnoticed that in spite of his objections to women participating in a shoot, Groupy had placed himself next to the two 'gels' in the line-up. Gels is, of course, the cultivated pronunciation of girls, in contrast to the earthy 'gals' of East Anglian country folk. We beaters were transported in 4 x 4s to the area of the estate which we were to drive, where a further briefing from ex-RSM Harry Jones made plain our duties. The position and route for each beater was stated in detail, so each drive would be conducted with near precision. Once at our posts, we heard the whistle blow and we were off waving our sticks. The first drive was across overgrown stubble towards a far hedge. Partridges began to rise and the guns to fire. The second drive was across a sugar beet field, the third in a scrub heath and the last of the morning through woodland.

The lunch break arrived far more quickly than I anticipated and we were ushered towards a pick-up containing refreshment hampers. It appeared someone had been using the pick-up for target practice, for a window was broken and the door and side of the vehicle liberally pocked by shot. We learned that one of the Hooray Henry guns had seen a fox put up and, disobeying good shooting practice, had lowered his 12-bore and let fly both barrels at the speeding animal. The fox escaped unhurt; instead the man's swinging aim had caught the pick-up full blast. Fortunately the refreshment hampers and contents appeared unharmed, until the perpetrator of the crime suddenly found a piece of shot in his mouth while munching a smoked salmon sandwich. The shot identified, the man went deathly white, informing us that he had already swallowed two pieces thinking it to be seed bread. Panic set in and he insisted on being carted off to a doctor before he died of food poisoning. The rest of us chewed carefully but it was found that only one pack of sandwiches had taken any harm. The irony of the situation provoked some acid if amusing comments, chiefly from Groupy. I noticed that he had become quite chatty with the young women, who seemed more than able to deal with the occasional sexist remark that came their way. After lunch the numbers of pheasant and partridge put up must have been twice the morning total. The winter sun hung unshrouded most of the time and the still air suggested we were in for a good frost come the night. Precisely at four-thirty Groupy's whistle brought the shoot to a close and we clambered on to the vehicles to be conveyed back to Woodborne Hall.

"You're expected to stay for the dinner. Drinks at five thirty and we'll sit down at six on the dot. No class distinction here, beaters and guns all round the same table," Groupy announced. And what a table! Twenty persons could easily sit comfortably either side, and at a pinch there was room for two at each end. However, the head of the table was only set for one, our host, and I was honoured to find my name on the plate to his immediate right. During the pre-dinner drinks Groupy approached me and asked if I had enjoyed my day. Following my assurance that I had, he came close and in lowered voice reviewed his prejudices:

"Told you I didn't hold with ladies totin' guns. Well, have to admit these two were a surprise. One knocked down twenty-three birds today and the other nineteen. Best any of we boys could do is young Peter there who bagged eleven. The rest were mostly in single figures, and all that damn young fool from Lloyds could do was knock down a couple of rooks. Said he thought they were black partridge: I ask you! Frankly, thought the gels would be a pain in the arse, not that they'd lick the pants off us. Chaps have had to mind their language and that'll put a damper on the dinner stories this evening. Things normally get a little fruity."

In the event, the proceeding cannot have been much subdued by the female presence. As the consumption of wine, spirits and beer mounted so did the exuberance of the diners and the anecdotes told were very fruity indeed. What was more surprising was that the young women who had put the men to shame with their day's bag, were also very willing to dispense fruity tales, all of which, I noticed, tended to mock males. Groupy, who didn't have to drive anywhere that evening, made good use of his own hospitality and while not drunk was certainly exceedingly happy. He proposed a toast to the ladies which was certainly fruity and received an equally fruity, yet far more subtle, acknowledgement from one of the girls. It was entertaining just to witness the skill with which these two Sloanes deftly deflected the various overtures made by several of the men present. In short, they were not for serious chatting up, but as happens on party occasions, there is always some blinkered man who does not get the message.

The 'gels' were the first to depart as they were driving back to London that evening. A few of the men from the City also took their leave of Groupy around the same time. When our host returned to the table after seeing these guests off, he leaned my way and with a twist of his moustache commented; "Fine looking gels. Clever too. Like a woman with a bit of wit. Forty years ago I'd have been after them like a shot. Gather they're in business together as the brunette said the blonde was her partner. Yes, have to admit I was mistaken about them."

He was indeed, but not in the way he meant. It was very obvious to me that the 'gels' were not the kind of partners he was thinking of. And I wasn't going to spoil his evening by enlightening him.

Josephine

Man calls himself human to acknowledge his supreme place in the animal kingdom where he exploits lesser species for food and welfare. Nothing amiss with this, for all life on this planet is sustained by the removal of other life forms. With his exalted position you might think man has it all his own way with the animal types he has used for his purposes over thousands of years. Not a bit of it, as I know from personal experience.

Take the dear, docile, old dairy cow, placidly chewing the cud, bearing calves to man's requirements and twice or thrice a day dutifully providing milk. The reality of a cowman's life is very different, his charges constantly endeavouring to outwit him when he least expects it. The cows and their regular charge eventually establish an uneasy truce, but woe betide the unfortunate relief milker. He is fair game for the full gamut of bovine shenanigans.

For many years I was relief milker to our small Frisian herd when Clive, the regular cowman, had time off or a holiday. The task was exacting because I have no doubt the herd, seeing the change of stewardship, went out of their way to be deliberately awkward. Like humans, cows come in a variety of shapes and sizes and with different temperaments. It did not take me long to discover that one particular cow definitely had it in for me. Her name was Josephine. I cannot now recall if she was reared on the farm or bought in, or, for that matter, who bestowed the name and why. All I can say is that if Napoleon had as much trouble with his Josephine, no wonder he finally lost out.

A large animal, relative to the rest of the herd, she had a coat that was more white than black, suggesting an origin not pure Frisian. Fortunately she was polled, otherwise I would probably have suffered more in the contest that arose. When it was my job to milk if a cow was reported to have escaped out into a field of standing grain or had broken into the meal shed, nine times out of ten it was Josephine.

Almost without fail when I arrived in the meadow to bring the herd to the shed for milking they would be at the far end. Calls only brought a line of bovine faces, eyeing my approach, but no hoof moved until I had laboured right across the field. Even then some would continue to stare or graze until approached with a stick, making off just in time to avoid a whack. It was soon evident that the chief adherent to this practice was Josphine, who was frequently the last of the bunch to move towards the cowshed. Her next ploy was to overtake several of the other cows so as to be one of the first into the collecting yard. Then, as the last cows also reached that point, Josephine would suddenly run back into the field, panicking one or two of the others, who followed. By the time I had eventually got all the cows into the collecting yard a high degree of exhaustion and irritation existed – but not with them.

Josephine had an alternative scenario for the winter months, when sugarbeet pulp and hay were put into the cow shed mangers prior to the herd being brought from the field. In contrast to the usual laggardly behaviour, she would shoot into the cowshed at the first opportunity and immediately set about devouring other cows' rations, occupying their positions so that when the rightful recipient arrived Josephine was in its place. Extracting the miscreant and getting her in the right place brought more confusion, with some cows trotting outside again. When all were eventually secured in their right places there was, to say the least, some personal relief. However, battle was far from over.

Unless they were nervous or upset there was never any problem with putting the milking machine cluster on most cows. Clive never had any trouble in this respect with Josephine; but I did. No matter how coaxing or careful my approach, as soon as all four teat cups were fitted and I moved away, the wretched animal would bring its right back leg up smartly to kick the cluster off. Sometimes it would take three attempts, extra meal in its manger and a retaining string round Josephine's girth before she would finally condescend to let the milk flow. It was almost as if she was showing me who was boss: the relief milker soon came to realise he wasn't!

Cow tails are for fanning flies and otherwise are a generally harmless appendage: Josephine's was an offensive weapon. Many was the time the mucky end landed smack around my neck or across my face when passing close by or attending to the cow beside her. Invariably the nice clean white milking smock would quickly be striped and flecked with slimey brown from Josephine's tail. Another trick when I had been to the manger was to move her bulk suddenly sideways, trapping me against the next cow. A good measure of slapping and cursing was required to get the beast to move herself back again. Josephine really excelled herself on the occasion when, in one of these sudden sideways movements, she cleverly managed to put a hoof right on top of my right foot. Figuring that the whole cow weighed a ton, my foot was supporting at least a quarter, although it felt like the whole lot. Perhaps only a few seconds passed before I was able to get the wretched animal to move, yet it felt like an hour. Everyone thought it extremely funny, except the victim who was hobbling around the farm for a good month. What was more difficult to endure was the fact that whenever I hobbled into the collecting yard or meadow that damn cow always appeared to be eyeing me with a look of contempt while chewing its cud.

Probably the most exasperating of all Josephine's behavioural traits was that which made so much unnecessary work mucking out. Turned loose after milking, cows are given to relieving themselves. When Clive was in charge this usually took place outside the cowshed in the collecting yard. When the relief milker was present the discharge invariably occurred in the cowshed, however quickly the cows were hurried out. It took me a little while to appreciate that the chain reaction was started by one cow. Yes, the dreaded Josephine. I tried keeping her tethered until last, but this made no difference as she simply started as soon as she heard the first cow released from its manger, and the rest of the herd all unloaded in sympathy. I tried milking Josephine early and releasing her well before the rest. That was worse, for she performed while still tethered, and so did the others. Shifting the residues from thirty-five cows takes a lot of time and effort. No one can convince me this was not a bovine conspiracy. Telepathic communication? Heaven knows.

The answer to all this aggravation would have been to send Josephine to market, except that she was one of the best milkers. And Clive never seemed to have much trouble with her, so what I had done to offend her was a mystery. All long ago now, and I guess that eventually Josephine ended up in tins of dog or cat food like most departed livestock. Some folk have nightmares about ghosties and ghoulies. If I have a bad dream it is of a cud chewing, bovine countenance, eyeing me with disdain.

A Pig In The Middle

There was a time when keeping a pig was something of a status symbol in a country village. A female reader may at this point be thinking that there are still plenty of rural pigs about if of dubious status, so I hasten to add that I am not referring to the human variety.

A backyard pig fattened largely on household scraps could provide a bountiful larder, although before deep freezers were a common domestic item there was too much meat at one go and most had to be sold or given away. Thus most backyard pigs were fattened for market, the remuneration received being a welcome addition to the generally low income of ordinary village folk.

When I was a lad backyard pigs were more common than dogs in this village. A dog, as now, costs money to keep: a pig could make money. To meet this practice there were individuals who kept breeding sows to supply the individual piglets weaned at about eight weeks. These were usually smallholders, the farmers who kept pigs on a commercial scale generally could not be bothered with the one here, one there trade. Besides, the smallholders who supplied the backyard pig market charged a lot less for their weaners than the average farmer.

In this district a weaner for the backyard sty could be had either from Albert Scrutts, our Rue's eldest brother, who lived in Chapel Hill Lane, or Jack Markwhite, the jobbing thatcher, of The Pightle on Longham Road. Over the years a good degree of competition arose between these two as various customers were in praise or otherwise of the progeny supplied, a situation largely brought about by Bill Stokes, who ran the village taxi. Custom for Stokes' large nineteen-thirties Wolseley saloon was often scanty, so he was pleased to use the vehicle to fetch and carry other than human passengers. One of these sidelines was carrying both Scrutts' and Markwhite's weaners in the car's boot to their customers. His charge was considerably less than that of professional carriers in the district, and we are talking about times when few of the villagers who had a backyard pig could afford a car of their own. In fact, as the standard of living improved over the years and the car became commonplace, so the backyard pig vanished from the rural scene.

Stokes' piglet haulage mostly involved separate journeys but there was the odd occasion when in the cause of economy he combined taxi work with these deliveries. As he was not in the habit of informing his fares what was in the boot and the partition behind the back seat was not particularly substantial, the muffled grunts and smells were disconcertingly attributed by one back seat passenger to the other.

Those who sought to rear a backyard pig would first visit Albie Scrutts or Jack Markwhite to make their selection, and then arrange for the recommended transport. The two breeders were both inclined to ask questions of Stokes as to the commercial welfare of the other, a habit which Stokes, for no other reason than to annoy, would delight in exploiting.

"What are Markwhite's litters like this year?" Albie would ask.

"Champion," Stokes would tease. "His three sows all had sixteen piglets each and he ain't lost none."

Albie's face darkened:"They won't be much good. If a sow has as many as that she can't do 'em well. They won't be good fatteners, that's for sure."

"You're wrong there. Nibby Tegget have one and he say he's never seen a pig put on weight like it."

"You never could believe Nibby. I bet that won't do well if that come from a big litter. Not enough tits to go round. You ain't a goin' to tell me his sows have sixteen apiece?"

"I ain't counted 'em. But reckon they have," being Stokes final comment as he slammed the driver's door of the Wolseley and brought its engine to life.

Such encounters had the effect of putting Albie Scrutts in a bad mood for the rest of the day, setting him hobbling around his ramshackle collection of buildings at an ever faster pace than usual. Albie hobbled because – he declared – of being shorter in the left leg than the right. A situation brought about – he said – by having spent the first thirty years of his life as a horse ploughman walking with his right foot in the furrow and the left on the unturned land. Indeed, whenever one saw him walking where the road was kerbed he no longer limped because he always had one foot in the road and the other on the kerb. Whatever the truth of the matter, despite the limp Albie always moved at a pace half as fast again as anyone else: crudely described by his brother as being 'like a fellow who has just dropped one and don't want the smell to catch up with him'.

Next time a villager wanted a piglet collected from Jack Markwhite, Bill Stokes would similarly wind up this supplier. If Markwhite didn't enquire of his competitor Stokes would quickly bring up the subject.

"Had to collect one from Albie Scrutts a fortnight ago for Comey Smith. He's got some champion looking piglets since he's been using Billy Hastings' boar."

"Billy charge too much to bring his boar. I ain't got no fault to f-f-find with Hurry Hadstock's." Jack Markwhite suffered an occasional stutter which got progressively worse as he became agitated.

"They say Hadstock over-work his boar and the litters by it are getting weaker. He's always cartin' it around. All very well tryin' to make a few bob, but that'll end up becomin' important – or whatever they call it when thas run out of steam. Just like old Fenney when he was tryin' to keep his wife, the gal at the grocer's and Edie Mortlake all happy at the same time. Blast, some mornin's he didn't hardly have the strength to stand up."

"I ain't got no f-f-f-fault to f-f-find with Hurry's boar. My piglets is f-f-fine." In addition to the stutter Markwhite's ears tended to redden with irritation. They were rather large ears for such a small angular face, which was also dominated by a Roman nose.

Stokes continued to nettle: "Well, I have to say Albie's weaners look somethin' good. A lot of people are goin' to him nowadays."

"W-w-well, I ain't h-h-ha-had any complaints. One of my last lot went to 170 pounds in twelve w-w-weeks! You ain't a goin' to t-t-tell me Scrutts can do any b-b-better? If so he's a f-f-f . . ."

Having secured the squiggling forty pound weaner in the boot, Stokes didn't wait for Markwhite to find further words and simply wished him a cheery good day and rumbled out of The Pightle yard amidst the usual cloud of blue exhaust smoke.

During the next visit to pick up a pig from Albie Scrutts good use was made of Markwhite's comment on how much weight one of a recent litter had put on in twelve weeks, only the details were exaggerated to cause the maximum upset.

"I was over Jack's a couple of days ago to collect one for a fellow at Wenham. Must say, by usin' Hurry Hadstock's boar he ain't half gettin' some good litters. He tell me he had one pig what he's kept and fattened himself put on two hundred pounds in eight weeks."

The permanent frown on Albie's walnut face deepened: "Well then he's a lyin' bugger. That ain't possible."

"Well I thought thas what he said. You know how he have that incurable stutter."

"I could tell him how to cure it. Keep his bloody mouth shut!" was Albie's disgruntled termination of the conversation.

Such was the provocation Bill Stokes caused, purely for his own amusement. Not wishing to do anything that might upset his trade, he was wise enough never to make any caustic comments about the suppliers or their produce to the customers. Yet for several years he continued to wind up Scrutts and Markwhite during his occasional calls to collect a weaner. As so often happens in such a situation, Bill Stokes became a bit too smug and over-confident.

In the hope of being in a good position to pick up extra taxi trade, Bill Stokes had got himself elected to the parish council. One or two of the more affluent village residents were also members and they and their friends were the most likely people to need and afford taxi service. To mark the five hundredth year of the village church a grand celebration fete was planned for the summer of 1961, which would also raise money for the upkeep of the church fabric. The councillors were fully committed to this project and each busied himself in various approved ways. Among the ventures for which Stokes had volunteered his services was the solicitation of various prizes for fete side-shows and competitions. At his suggestion one of the former should be Bowling for the Pig. He had already approached Albert Scrutts and Jack Markwhite for a prize piglet, to which each had agreed, he informed his fellow councillors. Of course, Scrutts and Markwhite had made no such offer, but Bill had no doubt he could easily bully them into these donations by his old trick of running one against the other.

There is, however, nothing so tight as a tight-fisted man, and both Scrutts and Markwhite worked hard for a living and were not going to give the fruits of their labours away to a fun fair. Stokes first tried the porky on Scrutts that Markwhite was giving one, so surely he would give a piglet, but this cut no ice. He tried using the good offices of the Church, which had even less effect, Albie not having been inside a church since he was married and holding it largely responsible for forty-five years of torment with a woman he had taken as wife. Having been rebuffed by Scrutts, the same tack was taken with Markwhite, who was equally unmoved and just as much a stranger in the church. Stokes finally had to retreat when Markwhite got onto the thorny subject of tithe and worked himself up into such a rage over the supposed avarice of the clergy that his f-f-f-fs and b-b-b-bs made his statements completely unintelligible. A few days later Stokes tried again, but for all his wily ways the answer from both men was a resounding negative.

Having given his fellow parish councillors to understand it was a certainty, Stokes now chose to go into reverse by saying that both prospective benefactors had changed their minds. The Chairman, Cecil Ludington-Witt, was not having this, as posters advertising the event mentioned Bowling for the Pig. Stokes managed to placate him by saying he was fairly certain he could obtain a couple of pigs elsewhere. To save face, Stokes was ready to put his hand in his pocket if no one would make a gift to the church fete. Alas, although he went to farmers as far afield as Bergholt and Hintlesham, none had any piglets near weaning age; all were either too large or too small. Meanwhile it was also Stokes' misfortune that Ludington-Witt should chance to see Albie Scrutts negotiating the kerb in the village street while on his way to The Wheelright's Arms for his weekly Saturday midday pint. In response to Ludington-Witt's accusation Scrutts quickly made it clear that no such promise had ever been made to Stokes. The wretched Stokes had to engage in some smart back-pedalling at the next council meeting, his only excuse being that 'there had been some misunderstanding' but he was still sure he could find the animals so that Bowling for the Pig could remain part of the fete programme.

Not a little amusement was caused when on the day it was found that Bowling for the Pig was for two brown and white guinea pigs, offered as one prize instead of the advertised two. There was even more amusement when they were won by Jack Markwhite.

The Local Law

In my youth horizons were not far beyond the parish boundary. Experience and knowledge of law and order went little further than the village policeman. Within his domain his word and deed were near to sacrosanct. Neither the vicar nor any other member of our local society had such commanding status. While we boys certainly did not go in fear of him, we were very conscious of his powers and authority, albeit they rarely went beyond a clip round the ear or a severe telling off as far as we were concerned. Even in the adult world our constable was rarely involved in a prosecution as there were never any misdemeanours in our rural patch serious enough in our policeman's opinion to warrant arrests and charges; he had his own way of combating crime and waywardness. Only in later years did I come to appreciate the degree to which PC Herbert would bend by dealing with offenders in his way.

Take drunkenness. There was a lot of it about, but I do not recall any 'drunk in charge' cases. He liked a regular pint himself, and rarely paid for it by all accounts. Being well aware of lapses in closing time at the Wheelright's Arms and the Anchor, he had his subtle way of letting the landlords know his disapproval and the means of obtaining a blind eye. A complimentary pint was often forthcoming when Herbert called in for some other reason, but never when the law was being broken. A regular trip round the pubs on his cycle just before ten in the evening enabled the heavy drinkers to be kept in check. He never entered, the evidence that came to his sharp ears was sufficient. If some known individual was heard to be suffering from an excess of alcohol then he would find the tyres of his cycle or car deflated. When this happened repeatedly the offender soon learned to walk to the pub instead of using his personal transport.

As for petty pilfering, Herbert aligned his nightly patrols to the agricultural and horticultural seasons. For example, he was rarely to be seen near the commercial orchards other than at apple scrumping time, and then it seemed he was always at hand. More serious theft - and all theft was serious in his view - was rare, for Herbert's sleuthing was a bold deterrent factor. In the twenty-six years that Herbert served this parish – from 1938 to 1964 – I can recall only three instances of major crime having confronted him. In comparison with what rates as major crime in the late twentieth century these may seem almost trivial. Relative to the peaceable nature of our parish in those years they were far from trivial.

There was the loss of Comey Smith's ferrets. A ferret may rate a joke to an urban ignoramus; to a true countryman the creature ranks high status. The poacher's best friend; the scourge of the randy rabbit, whose predilection to multiplication continually threatens man's larder. Once the crime had been reported Constable Herbert immediately set off to the abode of the most likely culprit, but found neither ferrets nor Nasty. He then made tracks to the Wheelright's Arms and had all customers lined up outside while he sniffed each one. Ferret smell is unmistakable and resists soap and water. Most of Herbert's sniffs took in the rank odour of digesting beer and honest sweat, but no one had a trace of ferret. He then repeated the procedure at the Anchor and the Lamb with similar results, although he did not know quite what to make of the young man who reeked of something he said was called Four-Seven-Eleven cologne.

Nasty, with his track record of finding things before they were lost, remained the chief suspect. Most of us, like Herbert, could imagine Nasty having met someone in a pub who wanted to buy a ferret, most probably in another parish. When Nasty did eventually appear he stank of petrol, one of the few substances that will overcome ferret pong.

"I tripped and fell when I were fillin' up Brigadier Venables' lawn mower - you know I do his lawns. Got half a gallon out of the can all over me jacket and trousers. Lucky I weren't a smokin' at the time," he told Herbert. The policeman probably wished the rogue had been smoking as it might have saved a lot of trouble in the future. As always, the case against Nasty was never proved and the ferrets never retrieved.

Nor was there a satisfactory conclusion to the next serious transgression which briefly brought the village national acknowledgement, if not in the way most residents would have wished. It all started when Alice Keswick went to take in her washing from the line after returning home from a day's charring. A large pair of voluminous navy blue knickers was missing. As the pegs had been put back on the line there was no doubt in her mind that the garment had been stolen. Enraged, Keswick made straight for the police house and demanded of Herbert that he investigate. While understanding her concern, the constable pointed out that he could not go round lifting her neighbour's skirts to see if they were wearing a pair of navy blue bloomers as she suggested. Keswick was always one to call a spade a spade; other women might be too embarrassed to report the pilfering of their underwear to the police, as proved to be the case when she became indignantly vocal about her loss during the following week of charring around.

"I ain't the only one. Mrs. Maggs has lost a pink pair: Mrs Bigsby-Crapes, that posh solicitor's wife, had two pair of them fancy camiknickers gone from her line, and the girl Barnaby has lost a little pair of black briefs that these young'uns wear nowadays, not that you'd think they'd worry 'cause that ain't much to lose from what I seen." Provided with this information PC Herbert began to take the matter more seriously. Thus encouraged, modesty was overcome and within a week he had amassed details from thirteen women who had lost knickers from their linen lines. The thefts took in all social classes and all variations of this garment.

For once being somewhat flummoxed, Herbert decided to call in outside help. The Inspector drove out from town, listened to Herbert's account and gave his advice.

"A fetish fellow. A penny-short-of-a-pound fellow. Can't help themselves. Harmless. Probably wearing them himself." He then went on to light up his pipe and spend the next half hour regaling Herbert with tales of his own experience with similar thefts, offering no advice whatever on solutions before departing. Herbert did toy with the idea of getting every man in the parish to drop his trousers, but felt such action might stir up more trouble than it was worth. Reluctantly, he came to the conclusion there was little to be done except keep an eye on linen lines. The Inspector having been called in, the local press were soon to know of these thefts and carried a column piece of interviews under the byline Where Is The Underwear? This was picked up by one of the more scurrilous Sunday nationals which ran a heading: Will They Nick The Knicker Knicker?

Meanwhile a state of near paranoia arose among the females of our parish, many refusing to hang out their smalls, and woe betide any unfortunate male who should cast his eyes towards a linen line. The crowning moment of this situation came when Mrs Cynthia Aidswell walloped Brigadier Venables' face in the post office because she said he asked her if she was knickerless. She refused to apologise when it was pointed out that he had not been addressing her but calling his young nephew Nicholas to look at some greetings cards. It is noticeable that – according to the church register – since then no one has been christened Nicholas.

Almost a month to the day that Alice Keswick had stormed up to the police house door, the Inspector informed Herbert that the local Oxfam shop had reported a woman plonking a brown paper parcel down on the counter and hastily departing without explanation. Inside were twenty-one neatly ironed pairs of knickers, drawers, panties or whatever one likes to call them. "Whoever he is, his wife or sister has found him out and put a stop to it. Shouldn't think you'll have any more trouble," he advised Herbert.

The only garment reclaimed was voluminous navy blue: "A workin' woman like me can't afford to go givin' clothes to Oxfam. 'Sides, I wouldn't sleep easy knowin' some other woman was a-walkin' about in my knickers," Keswick announced.

Constable Herbert's most demanding case occurred about eighteen months before his retirement, it required all his tact, guile and skill to solve. Like most village playing fields, our field could until recent times boast no public facilities. At football and cricket matches spectators who had to answer the call of nature made for the back of the high hedge at the pavilion end, and as it appears males are incapable of lending support to a team without heavily imbibing beforehand, fairly constant use was made of the screening hedge. While those seeking relief were hidden from the crowd, they were not from the windows of the houses up on the rising ground in the other direction. This provided Miss Hazlebrook and Mrs Burt with regular entertainment, but not the more sensitive Mrs Ludington-Wit and a couple of other 'foreigners' who had recently come to live in the village. Demands were made to the parish council that a toilet should be provided, and as the 'foreigners' had made a point of dominating the council the demand was met. There was the matter of finance; all the local authority would fund was the conversion of part of the existing sports pavilion. One end of this tar-board building was eventually fashioned to contain a Ladies and a Gentlemen to serve both the playing field throng and visitors to the village, but not without considerable opposition from those 'oldies' in alms houses close by.

"Thas all very well for them toffs up on the rise. They'd soon be a-shoutin' if people was always a-crappin' outside their front doors" was the acid comment of little Tommy Keswick, Alice Keswick's seventy-four year old uncle.

As old habits die hard, the council had the hedge at the pavilion end of the playing field cut down to tummy-button height, another act that did not go down too well with many villagers. The 'them' and 'us' contention, never far below the surface of village social life, was resurgent. We had our own version of Clochemerle. Then, two weeks after the toilets were opened the whole building burned down.

The fire brigade called in a forensic expert who pronounced arson. A strong westerly wind had been blowing that night and a patch of scorched turf and a crumpled litter bin on the west side showed just where the fire had started. This was serious stuff, and PC Herbert was quick to begin his investigation. He first approached the residents of the alms houses, starting with eighty-eight-year-old Bertie Bull, who lived in that closest to the conflagration.

"Now Mr.Bull, do you remember seeing or hearing anything unusual yesterday evening before the blaze?"

"I doesn't try to remember nowadays. I did so much remberin' when I were young me head is now so full I get a headache if I add more. So I can't be of help to yer, much as I'd like" was the feeble response.

Realising he wasn't going to get anywhere here, Herbert moved next door to little Tommy Keswick, but did little better.

"I didn't hear or see a thing, and even if I had I'd be thinkin' I should keep it secret", Tommy quipped.

"Ain't no point in keepin' secrets, Tommy. You want to spread 'em around so they do some good." But Keswick was no more to be encouraged than his neighbour.

In the third house lived old lady Barnaby who made out she was only seventy even if everyone knew she would not see eighty again. Once more it was made plain that the demise of the public lavatory was not mourned in the alms houses. However, Herbert had already been given some information which he hoped might make Ethel Barnaby less hostile.

"I have a witness who walked past here at about eight last night who saw you come out of your door, Mrs Barnaby."

"So I did. To put the cat out. That were that young fellow with a pony tail who live down the street weren't it? I saw him. Pity he ain't got somethin' better to do than go carryin' tales about old ladies, the good for nothin'. You know what you find under a pony's tail, don't you? Well thas what he is !"

The fourth and last dwelling in the row was occupied by Polly Dodds, sister of the famous Draughty Dodds and going on ninety-five. Herbert thought he would give her a try, although her hearing was now so poor he doubted he would get anywhere, which proved to be the case when he asked if she had noticed anything suspicious before the fire.

"I ain't got a fire. I'm centrally heated," she croaked.

The constable decided his time would be better spent elsewhere, despite a firm conviction that the crumbly quartet knew more than they would admit.

Going back to where the fire had allegedly started, Herbert examined the litter bin. It was made of aluminium and had some sort of top, now distorted through the heat. Then it came to Herbert that on the one occasion he had made use of the Gents the litter bin had been inside. How come it was now outside? Banging some of the mess of ash and charred wood off the lid, he was puzzled by the raised lip; he could not see what purpose it served. The sleuth went and got Nibby Tegget, whom the council employed to mow the playing field and keep an eye on the pavilion. Tegget confirmed that the bin should have been inside the Gents; but more interestingly the item which Herbert thought was a lid was actually the top from the matching cigarette bin which stood inside against the opposite wall. On the raised lip Tegget said there was the wording Please Put Your Cigarette Ends Here.

Herbert was elated. Someone had obviously removed the top off the cigarette bin, placed it on top of the litter bin and put it outside the entrance door against the tarred weatherboarding. Someone else had obviously thought the receptacle was for cigarettes and thrown in a fag end. The westerly did the rest. When he learned from Tegget that a few of the village boys had been seen to take shelter in the Gents on bad weather evenings for a crafty smoke, Sherlock Homes could not have been more pleased with himself. A few more enquires as to who the lads were and it was not long before Herbert's deductions were confirmed. It being a windy evening five youngsters had gone into the loo for a crafty smoke and two at least recalled putting the butts in the receptacle when they left.

It only remained to discover who fitted the cigarette bin top on the litter bin and moved it outside. The bin must also have been well stocked with combustibles, judging by the heat pocked wreckage. The culprit knew the boys went in to smoke, so it must be someone nearby. The nearest were the four crotchety OAPs in the alms houses. Herbert tried a further interrogation but got no further than the first time. Nevertheless, he was commended by his superior for his detective work.

A new pavilion and club house with public toilet was built with the insurance money. After all, it was an accident. Well, a case of accidentally for the purpose by persons unknown, if you see what I mean. The new pavilion was erected at the other end of the playing field, as far away from the alms houses as it could be on parish land.

Harry Newson's Holiday

"What do you think of the new vicar enterin' himself for the grand pricks?"

The woman two doors down, perching on a chair cleaning a front window, nearly lost her balance on hearing this outburst from old Newson. Lest there be further verbal sensationalisms of this nature I hurriedly crossed the road to his gate so that he had no need to shout.

"It's pronounced Gram Pree. It's French," I advised.

"Them French can speak it how they like but I'm sayin' it in English and thas how thas spelt! Anyways, I were askin' you a question."

"First I've heard about it. Somebody did tell me he drove racing cars as a pastime. Unusual for a clergyman. But then nowadays nothing surprises me," was my profound response.

"Reckon he's eager to get to heaven afore the rest of us, 'cause he stand a good chance beltin' around in those things. He's off to France next month so Mrs Keswick were a-sayin'. He's welcome; you won't get me near that place again!"

"I didn't know you had been to France," I queried. "When was that?"

"You ain't the only one what's been to foreign places," old Newson snapped. "I went when my Missus were still around; must have been about twenty-five or more years ago.

That were my daughter's fault, she kept on a-sayin' how as we should see the world and have a holiday. Holiday, I say, what do the likes of us want with a holiday. We don't need a holiday, thas for your la-dedah people, not for good honest country folk. In a weak moment we let her book us on one of them coach trips; stay for a night in France and back again. Holiday! Bloody torture, I call it!"

The woman two doors down was now cleaning her front window for the second time, having obviously misinterpreted old Newson's opening remarks and hoping to hear something juicy. She was going to be unlucky, for it was not the young vicar's standing that was under review but an account – exaggerated no doubt – of Harry Newson's sole venture into foreign parts.

"My daughter she say we don't have to worry about nothin' 'cause thas an all-in tour. Well, we was bloody near all-in by the time we got back. Never been on a ship afore. The captain he come over the loudspeakers and said 'We have a little bit of a swell today'. All I can say is I wouldn't want to get caught up in a whole one. Blast, that old ferry were a pitching up and down as soon as we got outside the harbour and people was a lookin' like me front lawn after a spring rain. Didn't pay good money just to see what others had had for their dinners. Luckily I'd took along a bottle of me mushroom and that saved us."

Old Newson's mushroom wine is the most potent vintage I've ever had the folly to try. The nearest thing to liquid dynamite. "How come?" I asked.

"A few swigs of that and you're rockin' wherever you be, so we didn't notice the ship a-tossin' about. Anyway when we get to this French place and back in the coach, the first thing I see is our driver is on the wrong side of the road. A fellow in the next seat he tell me not to worry as they all drive on the other side of the road over there. I say to my Missus we better watch out, that look like these Frenchies do everything the other way round. When we get to into our hotel room and she come out of the bathroom she say 'You're right Harry. The toilet flush squirt up instead of down'. Weren't no sheets on the bed, just an eiderdown thing. I ask the maid what showed us to the room what's happened to the sheets and all she say is Do Fay and point at the bed. If she's a meanin' what I think she is I'd a been tellin' her to shut her mouth, only she don't know what I'm sayin' any more than I understood her."

"Duvet", I explained. "They call it a duvet".

Old Newson gave me one of those scolding looks of his: "I call it daylight robbery when you pays good money and they ain't got any sheets to put on your bed. Anyways, the tour guide had told us to come down at seven for a meal. Well, I'm not use to findin' me way about places like that so when I see one of the maids I think the best thing I can do is point to my mouth. All she do is point to a door and say 'Wee'. I say no, I just had one, I want to eat. Anyway, we finally find the room and sit at a table. Thas all too posh for my likes. I'd rather have been at me old kitchen table any day. Well, this French fellow gives us one of these menu things what have a lot of writing, only thas all in French. So I lean over and ask the folk on the next table what was on our coach if they know what I'm a-pointin' to on the menu. They say "Frog's legs." I ain't paid good money to eat bloody frogs, so I points to the next line. They say that's snails. When they told me the next thing was a horse meat steak I say to my Missus we'll stick to bread and cheese. No sheets on the bed and can't afford to feed you nothin' better than frogs, snails and horse meat; thas a disgrace. And that ain't all. When we come down for breakfast next mornin' all we get is a few owd buns and we find this place can't even afford cups and saucers. We was havin' to drink coffee out of soup bowls, I ask yer! When we got back to Dover the Customs man say to me 'Have you anything to declare?' I say yes; 'I declare I ain't bloody well ever a-goin' to set foot outside of owd England as long as live!' "

"Sorry, you didn't enjoy the trip and the way the French do things," I consoled, starting to walk away. "Wouldn't you like to see another country if the opportunity arose?"

"No, I'm happy here. When it come to holidays I'd rather turn on me owd telly and look at that Jill Dildo a runnin' around the world for the BBC."

I didn't bother to correct him as I laughed and went on my way. The woman two doors down had finally got off her chair, having cleaned that window at least four times. She looked decidedly disappointed.

Epitaph For A Farmer

He had been around the farm for 63 years and then, suddenly, he was there no more. To those who worked with him, and knew him, the realisation that they would never see and hear him again was not easily accepted. For weeks, months, perhaps years, there would be that fleeting thought of what he would have said or done in such a situation;: only the great healer time will fade his memory. When the sadness and remorse death brings have mellowed, those who knew and worked with him are given to thinking of him in clearer terms, devoid of sentiment; to appraising his life; to defining his character; to wondering why and wherefore.

For centuries his forebears had farmed in Suffolk. He too might have worked the heavy soil of his native lands had not the depression of the 'twenties made arable farming a doubtful venture. Instead he settled in a village where well-watered pastures and a retail milk round offered better opportunity of being able to rub two pennies together. At twenty-one, newly wed, he milked the cows and delivered the bottles seven days a week, fifty-two weeks a year - and could never afford to be ill. The 'twenties were gone, and so almost were the 'thirties, before he ventured to put a plough into those pastures.

Though times had improved and his endeavours had shown fruit, it was still a full day and a full week. When he did leave the farm it was on business, a sale, or the annual trip to the Milk Marketing Board AGM where he invariably voted against the Board as a cautionary gesture lest they be too rash with their spending! But the roaring 'forties brought the U-boat; Whitehall said 'Speed the plough'. Grain flourished in his fields, fields that had not borne an ear of wheat since Napoleon stormed through Europe.

This farmer's doctrine of success was making do without. The binder clattered once more, and if it faltered he could restore its will to work with a few odds and ends from the scrap heap. This scrap heap was a coveted possession; no didicoy could induce him to part with the straggling assembly of broken-down implements and a thousand oddments collected with the years. "I won't sell any of it; you never know what might come in useful," he would say. And those who complained of the unsightliness were often forced to admit that what he said was fact. Many an implement continued life with a grafting from that jumbled collection. This knack of making do, of never buying new if it could possibly be avoided, was born of necessity in the hard-up 'twenties and thenceforth flourished. His standby was binder twine and wire. There was, it seemed, no limit to the use of these secure-alls. When everything else failed, these usually served his purpose. But if he excelled at improvisation he was no less adept at constructing new implements and buildings on a shoestring budget, whether it be a grain drier, a cowshed, or a simple gadget.

When his generation was born, the horse was the only real source of traction on the land. The new prosperity of farming brought mechanisation in full, and though eager to invest in the new machines he was certainly loath to see the passing of the cart horse. The last old mare was secreted away in a paddock at an extremity of the farm, where it was maintained in idleness for two years. Should one of his employees hint that such unnecessary maintenance would incur loss, he would respond with the familiar platitude "you never know when it might come in useful". It is said that a farmer cannot afford to be sentimental over animals; this he acknowledged, yet in practice his affection for animals had the better of his reason. Often when a cow was long overdue for the knackers he would tend it and only as a last resort reluctantly make that phone call. A standing joke was a lame hen: most would have unhesitatingly wrung its neck; but not he. In this case the ailing fowl was restored to health and, quite tame, spent its days travelling round the farm in the back of his van. Perhaps he understood that animals are not so far removed from man and deserve more sympathy than most of us bestow. Still, if a cow or pig was stubborn, especially first thing in the morning when he was apt to be a trifle irritable, it would receive as fair a crop of curses as any Irish navvy could supply.

His generosity with a packet of cigarettes was unmatched; his friends often estimated that he offered and gave away twice as many as he actually smoked. This cost him dear in another way, for such generosity was the indirect cause of at least two stack fires.

There are few farmers who do not delight in the utterance of proverbs gathered from long forgotten acquaintances. In Hitler's day, when we often craned our necks at the droning, sparkling formations above, he would remind us, good naturedly that there was 'some bloke up there looking after that: he doesn't need your help'. But perhaps his favourite saying concerned employees: 'It is no good expecting a fifty per cent man to work like a hundred per cent man, because there is no such thing as a hundred per cent man. So if you've got a fifty per cent man you've got nothing to grumble about'.

A good natured delight in what, expressed in modern idiom, would be taking the mickey out of people was another characteristic. A favourite pastime which gave his fellows much cause for mirth was his ability to keep up a running commentary on the faults and favours observed in passers-by (He was certainly as shrewd a judge of a shapely pair of legs as he was of a good cow). When it came to pet aversions the Tithe Redemption Committee filled the bill, and there were no qualms about not meeting its demands until prosecution was threatened. This imposition on the farmer caused him to see the clergy in an unfavourable light, and thus only baptisms, weddings and funerals would get him to a church. Yet, one can but feel that in his work he came closer to the face of God than most of us come in a lifetime of church going.

Who was this man? It matters not, for he could have been any one of a hundred working farmers from these parts; a generation that witnessed the greatest period of change in agriculture since man first learned to plough. So life goes on. Soon others will wonder who built the granary and cowshed with concrete and asbestos, as we wonder who raised the old thatched barn and dug the ditches in the 'Sixteen Acres'. Perhaps there is no better yardstick to assess him than his own; for if there is no such thing as a hundred per cent man, he was certainly on the right side of seventy five per cent.

WH